The Plan

TAWDRA KANDLE

Emmy Carter is a hard-working, no-nonsense woman. She's focused only on supporting her family and growing her pie business. Working weekend nights at The RipTide is just something she does to help pay the bills. When it comes to men—or love—she's not interested. Since the day her surfer-boy husband walked out the door to find bigger waves, Emmy's been determined never to give another man power over her heart.

Cooper Davis agrees. He's been married—and divorced—twice, and he's got no desire to make it a trifecta. He has his carpentry business, which is his passion, and his teen-aged daughter to keep him busy. The posse, his best friends since boyhood, tease him about finding the right woman. But Cooper knows she doesn't exist.

When Emmy and Cooper share a casual hook-up late one night, isn't a big deal. It's just a one-time thing. Until it isn't. And although neither of them will admit to themselves or each other that they want more, each encounter only brings them closer to the happily-ever-after they never planned to have.

Like it or not . . . it's all part of The Plan.

The Plan
Copyright © 2015 Tawdra Kandle

Cover/Interior Design by Champagne Book Design

ISBN: 978-1-68230-265-1

Dedication

To all the strong women in my life, both past and present.

"And though she be but little, she is fierce." Shakespeare

The Plan

Chapter One

Emmy

THE BEACH WAS BATHED IN *the soft pink light of late afternoon fading into twilight, and I turned my face toward the sky, eyes closed as the familiar salt air swept over my skin. Behind me, a strong, hard body was a warm presence, and muscled arms encircled me. His lips touched my neck, and I tilted my head, giving him more access so that he could—*

"Emmy!"

I jerked my attention back to the scene in front of me and the noise of the crowded restaurant roared over my ears. I cringed a little as I leaned forward to hear Seline, the waitress who was trying to get my attention.

"You okay?" She looked at me with one eyebrow raised. "You looked like you were a million miles away, and your head was all cock-eyed."

I bit back the smartass response I wanted to give and shook my head. "Just preoccupied. Sorry. What do you need?"

1

Seline rolled her eyes. "Five glasses of chardonnay for the wild women in the corner." She glanced at the table in question, and I grinned. One Friday a month, a group of teachers from the Cove elementary school met here for girls' night. I was grateful for the business, even if they stuck firmly to the same white wine order each time. Seline, who considered herself an amateur wine connoisseur, took it as a personal affront that they wouldn't even listen to her recommendations for trying something new.

"Coming right up." I began lifting wine glasses from the rack above my head.

"Loud tonight." Seline covered her ears. "And crowded."

I lifted one shoulder. "We're busy. It'll quiet down as soon as all the dinner people move out." I uncorked the wine and tipped it over the five glasses. Seline moved each one onto her tray as I filled it. Lifting it in practiced hands, she grimaced at me.

"I'll be back. Wish me luck." She turned and navigated the tables and people with the practiced ease of experience.

I moved down the bar, offering refills, picking up checks that had to be processed and plates that needed to be bussed. Once I was satisfied that everyone was taken care of for the moment, I stepped back into the kitchen where my two evening cooks were finishing the last few orders before we switched to offering only bar food.

"Crazy tonight, huh?" Aaron glanced at me as he scraped the grill. "I think I set a new personal best on hamburgers flipped."

"A crazy night is a lucrative night." I winked at the

younger man. "When we do the tip share, I think you'll be raking it in."

"Let's hope so." He used a rag to clean off the scraper. "Hey, it's eight-thirty, so I'm shutting her down. That cool?"

"Yup." I patted our other cook's back. Carey was only a little younger than Aaron; he'd recruited her out of our local vocational school last year. I was fairly certain she was nursing a massive crush on our chief evening cook, but she was painfully shy and didn't seem to be able to speak more than a few words to him at a time. "You doing okay tonight, Carey?"

"Oh, yeah. Thanks." Her blue eyes flickered to mine and then darted over toward Aaron. "Keeping busy."

"Good to hear." I stretched my shoulders. "I better head back to the front, before the natives get too restless. Why don't you guys take a break before the bar shift starts up?"

Aaron was already ducking out of his apron. "Good idea. We'll just take five out on the deck, okay, Emmy?" He punched Carey lightly on the shoulder. "C'mon. Let's get some air."

I shook my head as Aaron held the screen door open for Carey. I wondered if he saw the gleam in her eyes when she looked at him and wasn't interested, or if he was seriously that blind. Either way, it wasn't my problem. I had a strict no-meddling policy when it came to other people's love lives. God knew I was an idiot when it came to my own crap.

As I'd predicted, the last few dinner tables cleared out within the next fifteen minutes. I dimmed the lights and nodded to Gritt Kelly, our resident DJ for Friday nights. He winked at me and leaned into the mic.

"Hey there, guys and gals, how y'all doin' tonight?

3

Welcome to Friday night at the Tiiiiiiide!" He stretched out the last word, and the room erupted. I leaned my elbows on the bar, watching as the irresistible beat of music drew people to the dance floor. There was a nice mix of locals and out-of-towners tonight, which wasn't unusual for this time of year. We were on the verge of season: the first wave of spring breakers would hit next week, and then my Cove friends would stay home, not wanting to fight the crowds. We'd still easily hit capacity though.

A man I didn't recognize made his way across the room and pulled out a barstool. He caught my eye. "Hey. Can I get a beer? Whatever you've got on tap is fine."

I put on my professional smile and pulled out a mug, filling it carefully. "Sure. If you're interested, we also have some great local craft beers." I reached to a lower shelf for the laminated list and slid it across the bar to him.

"Thanks. I like to enjoy the local culture when I'm visiting." His brown eyes slid down me, and I swallowed back a wave of irritation. *He's a customer. Play nice.*

"Oh, where're you from?" I picked up a bar rag and began wiping crumbs onto my hand.

"St. Louis." He raised the mug to his mouth and took a healthy gulp.

"Ah, gateway to the Midwest. Known for the Arch and for being the starting point of Lewis and Clark's journey west." I shook out the rag over the trashcan. "You're a ways from home."

"I am. So you've been to St. Louis?"

I shook my head. "Nope, not me. I've never been outside

the great state of Florida." I shrugged. "I just read a lot. And I love travel books." I poured some peanuts into a wooden bowl and nudged them over to him. "What brings you to the bustling cultural center that is Crystal Cove?"

"I work for a pharmaceutical company. I had to make some calls at the hospital over the bridge, and someone at the hotel told me this was the place to be on Friday nights." He swept a glance over the restaurant. "Apparently he was right."

I grinned. "Yep, it's true. The Riptide is the most happening spot on the beach. At least on weekend nights. Come back tomorrow night—we've got live music. This weekend it's a country band out of Jacksonville. They're really great."

"Will you be here?" He leaned forward, and his eyelids drooped a little. I guessed he was going for sexy, but he only looked half-asleep.

"Oh, yeah. I'm here every Friday and Saturday night."

He raised his eyebrows. "Are you the owner? I heard the restaurant was owned by a hot chick."

Now my irritation was flaring into a nice mad. "A hot chick, huh? No, I'm not the owner. The hot chick's my boss."

One side of his mouth curled up. "But you still qualify."

Ewww. I stared at him for a full minute, long enough, I hoped, that he got the picture. I couldn't be outright rude to a paying customer, but damn, sometimes holding back took everything I had. To give myself a few minutes' reprieve, I moved down to the far end of the bar to take care of my other customers. I refilled some wine glasses and collected a few quick food orders before returning to my problem child, who'd finished his beer.

"Would you like anything to eat? Our dinner menu is closed for the night, but we still offer some basic bar food. Fries, onion rings, chicken fingers, nachos . . ."

"How about a plate of fries? Onion rings are my favorite, but probably not a good idea considering the plans I have for this evening." He smirked.

"Fries it is." I snagged his mug, now empty. "Another of the same?"

"Nah, why don't you pick me out your favorite craft beer? Something to get my juices flowing." He winked.

Double ewww. "Sure thing." I bent over the small fridge beneath the bar, aware that his eyes were on my ass. I had the urge to cover it, but I wouldn't give him the satisfaction. Instead, I chose the most expensive beer and stood to pop the top.

"Thanks." He lifted the bottle to me and took a swig, closing his eyes in appreciation. "Ah, that's nice." Setting it back on the napkin I'd just provided, he leaned in a little further. "So what time do you get off?"

I laughed without any humor. "Way past your bedtime, dude. I'm the manager on weekend nights."

He reached out to trail a finger over my arm. "Oh, I might surprise you. Remember, I'm on central time. And I've got a lot of stamina."

It was time to put an end to this. "Look, I'm flattered. Really. You seem like a nice guy." *Or not.* "But I've got someone waiting at home for me." *Okay, technically not true, but there were three someones who lived in my house, even if they weren't home at the moment.*

"We don't have to go to your house. I've got a perfectly

nice hotel room just over the bridge." His hand moved higher on my arm.

I stepped away, but the area at this point of the bar was narrow, and I bumped my hip into a sharp corner. Biting back an expletive, I gritted my teeth. "I'm trying to be nice. But honestly, dude, not interested." I put enough emphasis on the last two words that he couldn't miss my meaning.

But some guys just don't know when to quit. "Oh, come on. Local gal like you, how many chances do you get to enjoy an evening with someone like me? Why don't you let me broaden your horizons a little?"

"Pretty sure she said *not interested.*"

Behind the annoying guy stood a tall, familiar figure. Cooper Davis didn't seem intimidating on a regular basis. He was slim without being scrawny; the black shirt he wore clung to a broad chest and wide shoulders. He was usually pretty chill, but there was intensity in his bright blue eyes that belied his easy posture. And right now, those eyes were narrowed at the man who had his hand on my arm.

The customer eased back onto his stool, and I moved out of range, watching the two men closely. I trusted Cooper. He wasn't going to start anything, not in Jude's restaurant, but this other guy was an unknown. I groped in the back pocket of my jeans for my cell, just in case.

But obviously the salesman saw something in Cooper's gaze that made him second-guess any sudden moves. He rose slowly, keeping his hands up as though we were about to frisk him. Shaking his head, he reached for his wallet and pulled out two bills.

"No big deal. Shit, I don't need this. I was just trying to be nice to the locals." He tossed the money onto the bar and took a few steps away before he looked back over his shoulder at me. "Good night, sweetheart. Lots of luck living the rest of your pathetic life in this backwater."

I clenched my fists under the bar to keep from shooting him a gesture that I knew would be far from the image Jude wanted to promote. She would've understood why I did it, but she expected more from me. And hell if I was going to disappoint her.

He stalked away and out. I noticed that Cooper watched until the door slammed behind him before he sat down on the abandoned stool. He raised one eyebrow at me.

I ran a hand over my hair, sighing. Now that the guy was gone, I felt my shoulders relax. "Thanks, Coop. I appreciate it." I paused, struggling to put my feelings into the right words. "I had that, though. I would've tossed his ass in another minute. But thank you all the same."

He nodded, his eyes thoughtful. "Yeah, I figured. But he was pissing me off. Guys like that are assholes. Wears a suit, travels around, thinks he's the shit."

I pulled out a tumbler and tipped a bottle over it, sliding it to Cooper. "On the house. Your favorite—Balvenie DoubleWood." I lifted my glass of water and touched it to the scotch. "Thanks for being my hero."

Cooper raised the drink to sniff it and smiled. "You didn't have to do that." He took a sip and nodded. "Yeah, that's good stuff right there."

"I know I didn't have to. I wanted to." I leaned across to

collect a credit card from the lady sitting two stools down from Coop, ran it through the machine and returned it to her with two copies of the receipt and a smile of thanks. When I looked over at Cooper again, he was still savoring his scotch. "Want something to eat? I don't usually see you in here on a Friday night."

He lifted one shoulder. "Had a kind of shitty day, didn't feel like being shut in the workshop anymore. Most of the time, I can hang there for days on end, but tonight, it was suffocating me."

I nodded. I got that, although my line of work was completely different from Cooper's artistry. "Want to talk about it? I know it's a total cliché, telling the bartender your problems, but it's a classic for a reason, you know."

He rubbed one hand over the back of his neck. "It'd sound stupid to anyone else. I tend to let crap get to me that doesn't matter to other people."

I smiled. "Oh, I doubt that. Try me."

Cooper turned his glass in a circle on the coaster, staring down into the amber liquid. "I got this order about two months ago. Lady wanted a rocking chair for her grandson's nursery. I told her at the time what I recommended as far as design, for comfort and for durability." He spread his hands palm up between us on the bar. "She insisted she knew better—she'd seen something in a magazine. Fine. I give people what they want. She comes in to pick it up today and has her daughter—her pregnant daughter, the one who's going to be using the chair when her baby comes—sit in it, try it out. Of course it's uncomfortable. It's a fucking nightmare to sit in. So the lady pitches a fit and insists I do something to make it right. 'Do something.'" He shook his head, scowling. "I wanted to throw her out and tell her to go torture someone else or buy her chair at Ikea."

I chewed the side of my lip. "But you didn't."

Cooper sighed. "I didn't." One side of his mouth lifted just slightly. "Don't get me wrong. I've done it before, tossed people out and told them to stick it up their asses. But this one . . . the daughter's standing there with tears in her eyes, because all she wants is a place to rock her kid, and you could tell she was near the end and just done with it all. Plus she probably knows her mom's a raging bitch."

"So you told her you'd fix it."

"Fix it? I told her I'd make a whole new damn chair. But this time, they're getting what I know works, and hell with some stupid design. It means I have to push some orders back, work some extra hours when I didn't plan on it, but I'll get it done before she pops the kid out. They went away happy. But I'm pissed."

I held up one finger and delivered a plate of nachos to two guys sitting down the bar. On my way back to Cooper, I stopped to offer the sweet young couple sitting close together more wine, and when they declined, brought them their check. When I returned to the end of the bar, Cooper had polished off his drink.

"Another?" I lifted the empty glass.

He hesitated and then shook his head. "No, thanks. Maybe just a beer. How about that local one that Logan's been raving about?"

I bent again to the fridge, as I had a little while before, and once again, I felt eyes on my ass. This time I didn't have any desire to cover it. I took off the cap and set the bottle in front of Cooper before leaning back and crossing my arms over my chest.

"So I think you're right to be pissed. Cooper, you're an artist. What you do . . . how you make those things of beauty out of wood . . . it blows my mind. You have the kind of gift that people need to respect. If you tell a client that she needs to scrap her design and listen to you, she should. I mean, if I could do what you can, I think I'd go around all the time telling people to kiss my ass and take what I choose to give them."

Cooper laughed, but I caught the gleam of pleasure in his eye. "Jude and Logan would tell you not to encourage me. They say I'm too prickly as it is." He tipped the beer back, taking a healthy pull, and I watched the column of his throat move up and down. He had just the barest hint of beard there, under his jaw, as though he'd forgotten to shave that part of his face. It made him look dangerous.

"You're not. You're just selective about who you want to work with. There's a difference. Like I said, artists have that prerogative."

He stared at me, those blue eyes delving into my head. "Emmy, don't sell yourself short. You're an artist too, you know. I've tasted your pies. Those crusts are incredible."

I rolled my eyes. "Pie crusts are fleeting. They're nothing but flour and water. And of course a few secret ingredients that I can't share or I'd have to kill you." I grinned. "But they're hardly art. I make them, people eat them . . . and they're forgotten. What you make can survive for generations. It's lasting."

He didn't answer me right away, but he didn't drop his eyes from mine either. I stood for a few minutes in silence until someone called me from down the bar. I got caught up with cashing out a few checks, taking a few more orders and filling some drink requests from the waitresses circulating on the floor. I almost expected Cooper to be gone by the time I got back to him; on the rare occasions he came in during weekend evenings, he seldom stayed for more than one drink.

But he was still there when I made my way back. And his eyes were still trained on me.

"What time do you get off, Emmy?" It was the same question the irritating customer had asked me over an hour before, but coming from Cooper, it ignited the spread of unfamiliar warmth down my center.

"A little after midnight or so. Maybe a tad later, depending on how the crowd is. It's usually worse on Saturday nights, with the bands here. Gritt finishes his shift at eleven-thirty, so people usually take off after that." I was babbling, and that was so not like me. Once my mouth stopped moving, my leg began jiggling. I was pretty sure Cooper couldn't see it from where he sat, but he might start to wonder why it looked like I was convulsing. I pushed off the counter and picked up his empty beer bottle. "Can I get you anything else?"

He seemed to be considering that question as though it had great importance. Finally, he shook his head. "Can I just get some ice water? And maybe a plate of fries if you've got some to spare?"

"Sure." I filled a clean tumbler with ice and water, added a lemon wedge and stepped into the kitchen to plate some of the last batch of fries Carey'd just pulled from the oil.

"You guys can turn off the fryer and clean up. We won't have any more food orders tonight, I don't think." It was a little after eleven, and the crowd was already thinning a bit.

"Gotcha." Aaron was already loading the dishwasher. Carey moved around the kitchen, flipping switches to turn off all the appliances still running.

I carried the fries to Cooper and hunted on the shelf under the bar for a bottle of barbecue sauce that I set down next to the plate. He cocked his head.

"You knew about the scotch. And now the barbecue sauce. How did you know that's what I eat with my fries?"

I hoped my face wasn't turning red. "I'm gifted at remembering customers' preferences. It's part of the bartender code. I can't tell you anything else, or again, I'd have to kill you."

Cooper laughed. "Like with the pie crust recipe? You, Emmy Carter, are a woman of many secrets."

Now I was certain I was blushing. "Yep, that's me. Woman of mystery."

He picked up one fry and dragged it through a puddle of barbecue sauce. "Tell me, woman of mystery, where are your kids tonight?"

My heart thudded against my ribcage, but I kept my voice cool. "They spend the weekends with my mom and dad. I dropped them off after school today, and I'll pick them up Sunday morning when I wake up."

Cooper nodded. "It's great that you have your folks to help."

"Yeah." I couldn't agree more. "I never would've made it this far without them. Well, and Jude and Daniel."

"Bullshit, Em." Cooper's words were heated, but his tone was mild. "You pull your own weight. I've seen it. Yeah, you've had some people give you a hand, but you'd have made it even without that. You're strong."

I blinked back an unexpected rise of moisture in my eyes. I never cried. It was a weakness I couldn't afford. "Maybe. But I'm glad I never had to test that theory yet." I wiped the bar down, careful to keep my focus on the rag. "Why'd you want to know about the kids? Were you going to call child protective services on me if I'd left them at home to fend for themselves?"

"No." Cooper spoke low, and I stopped moving so that I could hear him. "I wanted to know if your house was empty. And if maybe . . . you'd like some company after you finish here."

My mouth went dry, and my knees began to shake. I started moving the rag again, but I wasn't really seeing what I was doing. "I, um . . ." As inspired responses went, it was pretty lame.

"Emmy, saying no is perfectly acceptable." He reached toward my arm, his fingers stopping just short of touching me.

"I know that." I jerked up my chin to look at him. "I don't want to say no. It's just that I've been saying no for so long, I've kind of forgotten how to say yes."

A slow smile spread over Cooper's face. "I think you just did."

The waitresses and the busboy all left almost as soon as I'd locked the door behind the last departing customer. They paused only to pool and divide their tips, making sure that Aaron and Carey got their share, too. Once all the money had been recorded and distributed, the two cooks tossed their aprons into the laundry barrel and said good-night, too.

I noticed that Aaron's eyes lingered on Cooper where he still sat on the barstool, waiting for me. But he didn't say anything as he held the door for Carey and disappeared into the dark.

"What do you need to do to close up? How can I help?" Cooper stood and stretched, and his T-shirt rode up a little, giving me a tantalizing tease of the tan skin on his stomach. A well of want bubbled within me. *Down, girl.* I closed my eyes. *At least until we get home. Don't want to jump his bones in the restaurant.*

"I just need to make sure everything's turned off in the kitchen. Carey and Aaron are usually dependable about doing it, but a third set of eyes never hurts. Then I have to run a register report and lock up the money, do one more walk-through, turn on the safety lights and the alarm, turn off the regular lights and lock up behind me." I grinned. "Now you know all the secrets of shutting down the Tide."

Cooper pressed one hand to his heart. "It'll go with me to the grave. And don't worry, you still have plenty of other mysteries to hide from me, if you count the pie crust and the

ForCanBeConverted

bartenders' code." He cast a glance around the empty restaurant. "How about I do the kitchen check and walk-through while you take care of the register? I'll meet you at the door in ten minutes."

"That works."

I went through my routine, conscious at every turn that Cooper was nearby, moving with the typical grace that somehow only made him more masculine. He whistled under his breath, touching the grills and leaning over the deep fryers to check for residual heat. I tried to concentrate on setting up the register report and bagging the cash to put into the safe. Jude would send it to the bank first thing in the morning; we'd decided a long time ago that it wasn't safe for me to make night deposits by myself.

"Found this in one of the chairs." Cooper leaned against the bar, dangling a small pink purse from one finger. "And this in the ladies' room." He brought his other hand up. A black high heel rested on the palm.

"Oh, yeah." I sighed, shaking my head. "Can you toss the shoe into the lost and found box under the counter? I'll check the bag for ID."

"Don't bother. I already did, and it only has some play money and crayons. Reminds of something Lex had when she was little."

"Ah, okay. Lost and found then. I bet it belongs to Shana Hayes' little girl. They were in tonight for dinner."

Cooper came behind the bar with me and pulled out the crate that held a bunch of mismatched objects. He dropped the shoe and the purse into it and then reached back in, frowning. "Hey, this is my hat. I've been looking for it." He held up a bright green baseball cap that had clearly seen better days.

I rested my hip against the counter. "Do you have any proof that's yours, sir? I mean, we can't just let people take whatever they want willy-nilly from our lost and found box. Maybe that belongs to someone else."

He narrowed his eyes at me. "This is my favorite working hat. I've got pictures of me wearing it."

I stepped a little closer. "You have them on you?"

One side of Cooper's mouth quirked up. "Nope. But you're welcome to search me."

"I might." I slid along the bar until I stood just inches from him. "But not here. I need to close up . . . and I promise you, my house is much more comfortable than the bar."

His eyes fastened on me, fathomless and unreadable. "I'm willing to trust you. But maybe both of us could use a taste. Just to whet our appetites."

I was pretty sure my appetite was already incredibly whetted, but I didn't move. Cooper raised one hand to the side of my neck, touching the warm skin that was damp from a solid eight hours of moving around the bar. He curled his fingers, putting just the slightest bit of pressure at the base of my head. His thumb stroked beneath my jaw, and I shivered.

His lips twitched, but he didn't speak. He stared into my eyes for a moment before dropping his gaze to my mouth. Instinct kicked in, and my tongue shot out to run over my bottom lip.

Cooper raised one eyebrow as he watched me. When I didn't look away, he lowered his face toward mine and brushed my mouth with a touch so light I might've thought I'd imagined it. My eyes drifted partway down as he leaned closer, his lips nibbling at the corner of mine. I held my breath, just waiting for him to make the final shift to take my mouth.

But Cooper wasn't in any hurry, apparently. He moved to the other corner of my lips before he feathered another light caress over them. Just when I thought I might go completely crazy with wanting, he dropped one hand to my lower back, pressing me against his body, and gripped my chin with the other hand. I raised my eyelids just enough to see the blaze of want on his face before he consumed me.

This time, this kiss . . . there was nothing light or fleeting about it. Cooper's mouth so utterly took over mine that I couldn't feel where I ended and he began. His lips were firm and insistent, and when he tugged on my chin, I opened my lips without hesitation. A small sigh that ended in a groan escaped without me even realizing it came from my throat. My hands rested on his chest, between us, and I felt his heart pounding under my palm.

His tongue stroked over me, teasing, testing, and then bolder. He traced the outline of my lips before sucking the lower one between his teeth, biting gently. The hand on my back urged me even closer to him as his tongue made enticing plunges into my mouth, leaving no part of me untouched.

"Emmy." Cooper leaned his forehead against mine, his breath warm and rapid over my face as he murmured my name. "If we don't leave now for your house, I'm going to suggest we make use of that apartment upstairs. And I really don't want to do that."

"I just need to set the alarm and lock up." My hand closed on his shirt, gripping it to keep from falling over. "You should go out first, and then I'll be right behind you."

"Okay." He kissed me once more, hard and fast, before he let go of my back and my neck. I focused on not staggering as I turned around to punch numbers into the keypad for the alarm.

"Four-eight-seven-three." I said the numbers out loud as I typed them onto the pad, mostly to keep myself from jumping up and down and screaming, *Cooper Davis just kissed me!*

When the light began to blink its countdown, I slung my handbag over my shoulder and went outside, slamming the door behind me to make sure it was secure. Cooper stood at the bottom of the two steps that led from the parking lot to the door, and I hoped he didn't notice how my fingers shook while I locked the deadbolt.

"I'll just follow you home, if that's all right." He leaned against the railing of the steps.

"That makes sense." I nodded. "Do you . . . know where I live? Just in case you lose me?"

He grinned and raised up on one step, close enough to me that I could make out his intoxicating scent: sawdust, along with something that was even more uniquely Cooper.

"Yeah, I know where you live, Emmy. But even if not . . ." He glanced over his shoulder at the empty streets behind us. "I think I can manage to tail you this time of night." He reached up with one finger and tucked a strand of hair behind my ear, and when he spoke again, his voice was low. "Don't worry, I would never lose you."

Parts of my body that had been neglected for way too long began to stir to life again, and I wondered what he'd do if I pulled him to ground right there in the Riptide's parking lot.

Hold it together, woman. You can do better than that. Play it cool.

I attempted a laugh, something light that would make Cooper think I was used to this kind of hook-up—not that I was, and I definitely didn't want him to think I was a slut. I just needed to seem more sophisticated than I really was. Not plain old Emmy Carter who'd never left her home state and probably never would.

But the laugh ended up more like a breathless giggle. I covered by hiking my purse higher on my shoulder and jingling my car keys. "Okay. Good. I'll see you there in a few minutes then."

Cooper stood aside to let me pass, but as I walked to my van, I realized he hadn't moved toward his car. Instead, he watched me until I'd unlocked the door and climbed into the car. Only then did he push off the step and head to his Jeep.

I started up the van and maneuvered slowly to the exit of the lot, watching in my rear view mirror until Cooper's headlights shone behind me. Turning right, away from the ocean, I focused on keeping my speed a happy medium: not so fast that I'd seem like I was too eager to get home and not so slow that he'd think I was an old lady driver.

With the season not quite underway, the roads really were deserted this time of night. I always liked my ride home;

it gave me the perfect amount of time to unwind from the intensity and busyness of the restaurant, so that by the time I pulled into my own driveway, I was ready for a glass of wine, a half hour of mindless television comedy and then my bed.

Tonight, though, nerves jumped in my stomach, and my hands were sweaty on the steering wheel, all because Cooper Davis was driving behind me. Cooper Davis was following me home. Cooper Davis had *asked* if he could come home with me, and if I'd had any doubts about what that meant, he'd wiped them all away when he'd kissed me in the restaurant.

I didn't make a practice of bringing home guys. To be completely honest, I'd never done it. There just wasn't enough time or energy in my life to complicate it with men or even random sex. Between my kids, my parents, the house, my pie-making business and the hours at the Riptide, sex had fallen far down on my priority list. It was somewhere below meaningful adult conversation, which was something else that didn't happen often.

Now that I thought about it, that was just sad.

But tonight I was breaking my rules, because, well . . . *Cooper Davis.*

We'd both grown up in the Cove, so of course I'd known him all my life. Cooper and his friends were all older than me, though, so he wasn't really on my radar until I was in eighth grade. During the last week of school that June, our whole class had gone over to the high school for our orientation. We were supposed to learn how to navigate the bigger building, familiarize ourselves with the brand-new lockers and get an idea of what the next four years would hold.

We were split into groups for a tour of the school, but somehow, I got separated from mine when I stopped to get a drink at the water fountain. One minute they were all there, as our student guide bubbled enthusiastically about all the extracurricular activities Crystal Cove High would offer us, and the next minute, when I looked up from the water, dabbing at my face with the sleeve of my sweater (the high school was air-conditioned, so we'd all been warned to dress accordingly), they were gone. Vanished into thin air.

I wandered the hallways, peeking into classrooms and darting away fast so that no one spotted me and asked what I was doing. Our junior high teachers had put the fear of God into us about punishment in high school, and I could just see it now, printed on my permanent record: *Got lost and walked hallways without supervision.*

Retracing my steps seemed like the best idea. I was pretty sure we were all supposed to end up in the school gym, which was close to the front doors. If I could make it back there, maybe I could skulk until another group passed, and then just join them.

I turned the corner into the hallway I'd just come from and ran smack into a hard body.

"Whoa, there." Large hands caught my shoulders and steadied me. "Sorry about that. I didn't expect anyone to be coming around here."

My face was hot, which probably meant it was bright red, too—the curse of redheads. I wasn't afraid of boys, but this was no middle schooler—this was a high school guy.

"Sorry—I just was trying—" I stumbled over the words, my voice croaking like an old bullfrog.

"Are you here for orientation?" He sounded kind, not snooty like other older kids, so I risked a glance up at his face.

And that was it. I was a goner. My mouth went dry, my heart thudded hard and fast, and I lost all feeling in my hands. He was gorgeous. Vibrant blue eyes smiled down at me beneath black hair that was just a little too long—not girly, definitely not, but longer than most guys wore theirs. It skimmed the tops of his eyebrows, and I had the sudden insane urge to reach up and brush it back.

I recognized him then. I'd seen Cooper Davis hanging around the Riptide with the owners' kids when I went there with my friends over the summer. But then they were just a bunch of high schoolers, people I didn't need to know. Now I realized I'd never again see Cooper as just part of a crowd. He'd always stand out to me.

All of this buzzed through my brain at lightning speed, and some more aware part of me remembered he was still waiting for an answer. And still holding my shoulders. I could feel the heat of his hands through my thin sweater.

"Um, yeah. I guess I lost my group. I stopped for water and they must've gone in somewhere or something." To my own ears, I sounded hopelessly immature.

But Cooper just grinned at me as he dropped his hands. *Dang, I wished he'd kept them there a little longer.* "Yeah, it happens. Want me to help you find them?"

What I wanted was for Cooper to stay here and keep talking to me, just so I could listen to his voice. But that request would've seemed weird, I decided. "If you can maybe just point me to the gym, I think I can catch up with everyone there."

He drew himself up, taking a half-step back, and I had to crane my head to see his face. *Gosh, he was tall.* "I'll do better than that. I'll take you there." He started walking and added over his shoulder, "You get the special private Cooper Davis tour of Crystal Cove High. Don't tell anyone. It's an exclusive service."

I followed him, hardly hearing a word he said, with my head spinning and my heart practically singing. *Cooper Davis was walking with me, ME, Emmy Graham, in the halls of the high school, and maybe once we got to the gym, he'd ask for my phone number and then he'd call me and we'd date over the summer, and then come fall I'd be the only freshman who was dating someone who'd already graduated. And when I graduated, we'd get married and live in a little house right on the beach and raise pretty black-haired, blue-eyed babies. 'Cause I didn't want any of them to have my ugly red hair.*

"Here you are." Way too soon, we were back in the lobby, standing just outside the doors to the gymnasium. Kids from my own class were converging here, too, climbing onto the bleachers. I spied my own group already sitting down, so clearly I hadn't missed much in the tour.

I looked back to say thanks to Cooper. I had a speech prepared in my head, wherein I would introduce myself and offer my hand so that he'd be forced to touch me again. But he'd already turned around, and a pretty blonde wearing a short skirt and a skinny tank that showed off her big boobs had caught his attention. She had her hand on his arm and was whispering something in his ear, something that made his eyes crinkle in amusement. As I watched, fascinated and horrified, he brought his hand up—the same hand that had touched *me*—and rubbed her back, pressing her upper body closer to his.

I wanted to cry. I wanted to sink into the floor. And I wanted to scratch her eyes out.

Instead, though, I let the crowd push me into the gym. Taking a seat with my classmates, I dared one more glance out into the hall, hoping Cooper might've noticed I'd disappeared. But of course he hadn't. I wasn't even a blip on his radar as he wrapped both arms around the girl and dropped his head to nuzzle her neck.

I didn't see Cooper again until one of my friends dragged me to a baseball game right after graduation. The high school team had been on fire that year, making it to the playoffs, and Cooper played first base. I watched him from the safe anonymity of the stands, lusting after him in my heart as only a fourteen-year old girl can do. After that, I made it a point to be at every home game until Crystal Cove was eliminated.

For the rest of the summer, I satisfied my Cooper cravings by hanging out at the Tide much more than I ever had before. He was there fairly often, usually with other kids I came to identify as Matt Spencer, Eric Fleming, Daniel Hawthorne, Mark Rivers and Logan Holt. They were all hot guys, for sure, but none of them made my knees go weak like Cooper did. I tried to play it cool, but I was pretty sure there were times when he caught me staring, no matter how nonchalant I thought I was.

When autumn rolled around, all of my attention and time was sucked into adjusting to high school. Cooper went off to college in North Carolina on a baseball scholarship, and I heard through the grapevine that he was doing well. But in a young girl, absence doesn't always make the heart grow fonder, particularly when the love is unrequited. Cooper Davis faded into a sweet memory.

By the time he came back to Crystal Cove for good, after he'd injured his arm and lost his scholarship, I was already dating a cute surfer. The week after I graduated from high school, Cooper Davis married a girl he'd met in college, and I remembered feeling a pang on their wedding day, as though I'd lost something that had never really been mine.

For the next ten years or so, as I moved into marriage with the cute surfer and then quickly into motherhood as well, I was vaguely aware of Cooper's life, even though our paths almost never crossed. He and his wife had a daughter, but they divorced before she was very old. I knew Cooper had finished his degree at a local college and had opened his own carpentry business that morphed into artisan-style custom furniture. He married again, briefly, and I'd heard rumblings that wife number two was kind of a nut job, but I never met her.

When my own life imploded and I'd started the pie business out of sheer desperation, Jude Hawthorne was one of the first people to stand with me. She bought my baked goods for the Tide, and on the day I marched in and on pure bravado pretty much demanded that she bring me on as a night manager on weekends, she hardly blinked before hiring me. Working at the restaurant, I'd come to be friends with Jude and by default, the rest of her group. The men called themselves the posse—had since they were boys together. Before too long, they considered me part of them, or at least part of the female contingent, which included Mark's and Eric's wives as well as Jude.

Being friends meant I was included in their parties and impromptu gatherings. I began to see Cooper on a regular basis, and while he never treated me any different than the other guys did—I often felt like their surrogate little sister—I couldn't help remembering my massive crush on him. Time hadn't hurt Cooper's looks one bit. If anything, he'd filled out a little more, and the muscles on his arms still made my mouth go dry. Daydreaming over that man became one of my few guilty pleasures in a life that was filled with responsibility and worries.

But now Cooper Davis was pulling into my driveway behind me. He was shutting off the engine of his Jeep and climbing out. In a minute, he'd be inside my house with me. Alone.

I wished I could go back in time and high-five fourteen-year old me for what was about to happen.

Chapter Two

Cooper

EMMY'S HOUSE REMINDED ME OF the woman herself, I thought as I pulled into her driveway. It was small and neat, well-maintained without being flashy. It was the kind of place that might not catch the eye right away, but that had a kind of welcoming charm all its own.

I'd known of Emmy Carter in that vague way people are aware of those who surround them without really interacting. She was quite a bit younger than my usual group of friends, and since she didn't have any siblings in my class, we didn't have that connection. I'd known her ex-husband a little better, only because he'd worked for my friend Matt Spencer off and on a while back. Eddy Carter had made his name as an amateur surfer while he was still in high school. He was a minor celebrity in the Cove for that, but when his fame died out, it seemed his ambition did, too.

For the next five or six years, Eddy had ambled through

a series of short-term jobs, never sticking anywhere too long. I didn't think anyone was surprised when one day he up and left the Cove to move to Hawaii.

I remembered Jude's righteous indignation when that had happened. I'd been sitting at the bar around lunchtime, watching her slam things around. Sadie, the old woman who'd worked at the Tide probably since the time of Moses, muttered under her breath about good-for-nothing men. The way she glowered at me, as though I were to blame for my whole gender, made me slump down on my stool.

"Just . . . left. Like he didn't have a care in the world. Like he doesn't have a wife and three little kids depending on him." Jude shook her head. "Men."

Matt was sitting with me, and he slid me a look. "Eddy Carter. Took off for Hawaii yesterday, told the wife he was going to find bigger waves. All the women are on the warpath today. You've been warned."

I nodded. "Asshole move. Isn't he married to Emmy Graham? She always seemed like a decent chick. Not cool, what he did."

Given how Jude felt about the whole situation, it didn't surprise any of us when she announced a few weeks later that she was now buying all her pies for the Tide from Emmy, who'd started up a business out of her house to keep from going broke. A couple of months after that, Daniel told me that Jude had hired Emmy as her night manager on weekends.

"Could've knocked me over with a feather. I never thought Jude'd give up an ounce of control over this place. It's like her baby. But she said what Emmy suggested made sense, and she'd love to have a little more time with the kids and me on weekends." He'd sipped his beer and grinned. "Now if I could talk some other needy person into convincing Jude to let her take over the early morning openings, my life would be just about perfect."

Like that was ever going to happen. But for a good solid year, Daniel had a little extra time with his wife, the love of his life. They took a few trips and even went camping with the kids every now and then. When he was diagnosed with cancer and we all knew how bad it was, having Emmy around to help was even more important. Jude told me more than once that it gave her peace of mind to know there was someone she could call to take over at the Tide in case of an emergency, someone who already knew how everything worked. Any of the posse would've jumped in to help her without hesitating, but even though we'd been hanging out at the beach restaurant since we were all kids, we didn't know how to open it up or close it down, or the codes to the register and the alarm system. Emmy did, and she evolved in a sort of second in command.

The day of Daniel's funeral, we all gathered at the Tide after the service. I made it through about forty minutes of agonizing small talk before I had to get out. I grabbed two bottles of beer from the big tub of ice and snuck out onto the deck.

The day was gray and damp, a little unusual for autumn in Florida, but it felt right for today. It fit my mood. I headed for the far end of the wooden platform, planning to lean over the railing, watch the ocean and drink my beers. Grief made me seek solitude.

But I wasn't alone out there. A slimmer figure was already in the exact spot I'd intended to take, resting her elbows on the wide rail. I knew it was Emmy, because I'd taken a sort of distracted notice earlier of the dress she was wearing. It was black and hit her around mid-calf, and she'd paired it with black strappy sandals. When I'd seen her coming up the aisle of the church that morning, I realized that I'd never seen Emmy Carter in a dress. Shorts, yes; they were her regular uniform at the Tide. Jeans in the winter, sure. But never anything dressier. She looked completely different, and it took me by surprise.

She heard my steps and glanced over her shoulder. I paused, surprised at the stormy expression on her face. A single tear riveted down her cheek, but her brows were drawn together and her mouth tight.

"Hey." Emmy's voice was rough. "Is everything okay? Did you need something?"

It struck me that Emmy was always asking that kind of question—how could she help? What could she do? She'd been frenetic during the last few weeks of Daniel's illness, cooking, handling the Tide, helping with rides to the hospital . . . and never once had I seen anyone ask her how she was doing.

"Nah." I shook my head. "I was just getting sensory overload in there. Too many people, too much emotion and not enough space. I was looking for some quiet."

"Ah. Sorry about that." She pushed to stand up. "I'll leave you to it."

"Emmy." I put my hand on her arm, curling my fingers

around her small bicep. "Stay. I can have the quiet with you here."

She laughed, a bark of sound that was barely related to humor. "I wouldn't be so sure of that. I'm not feeling very quiet. And sure as hell not feeling the peace."

I frowned. "What's wrong?"

"What's *wrong?*" Emmy stared as if I were insane. "What's right would be a better question. There's nothing but wrong about today. It's a big foaming bucket of fucking wrongness." She leaned her back against the deck guard. "This is not how things were supposed to be. Jude and Daniel were supposed to be the couple who made it. They were supposed to be together to the very end, 'til they were both old and sitting out here with big old hats and canes. They were supposed to see their kids grow up and get married, and then enjoy fat grandbabies. And great grandbabies." She kicked against the wood post as though it held responsibility for all the ways life had wronged us. "But no. Instead we all watched Daniel waste away to practically nothing over the last year, and now he's gone. *Dead.* And Jude's alone, and her heart's broken, and I don't know why this kind of shit happens. It wasn't supposed to happen to her. Not to Jude and Daniel."

She swallowed, and I could tell by the way her mouth was working that she was on the verge of crying. Maybe that was what she needed, I thought. I sure as hell didn't have any answers for her.

"Here." I thrust one of the beers in front of her. "I don't know if this'll help, but it's a start."

Emmy stared at the bottle for a minute and then took

it. "Thanks. God knows it couldn't hurt." She took a long swig, the slim column of her throat moving up and down. I watched, fascinated. After she lowered it from her mouth, she used the back of her hand to blot her lips. Her hazel eyes flashed up to mine, and there was a little less pain in them.

"Better?" I took a pull of my own, my gaze staying on hers.

"It's a start." She repeated my words back to me and then sagged back against the railing. "Hey, Cooper, I'm sorry. You're probably thinking I'm the biggest whiney wuss you ever saw."

I quirked one eyebrow. "Um, why would I think that? You're understandably pissed off at the injustice of life." Something occurred to me at that moment, but it wasn't the time to bring it up. Not when she was just settling a little. "Pretty sure we're all feeling that today. You're just expressing it better than most of us."

Emmy shrugged. "But I don't have the right—I mean, I loved Daniel. He was a good friend, and he was kind to me, and he and Jude practically saved my life when they gave me a chance at the Tide. I'll never forget that. But I only really knew him the last few years. You all have been friends since you were kids. I didn't mean to act like this is worse for me. I should be bringing you beers, not the other way around."

"Bullshit." My tone stayed even, and I took another drink. "Friendship isn't measured in time, Emmy. You might not've known Daniel as long, but that doesn't mean your pain isn't just as deep. And valid. Plus, you've been running all the hell over the place for months now, trying to make sure everyone's taken care of. How many meals did you cook Jude? How often did you drive the kids to the hospital or to the airport, when they were running back and forth? It's okay to let go a little now, Emmy. You're human." I moved to take up my spot next to her, staring at the churning blue-gray foam beneath us. "You just said exactly what we're all feeling. It's what I needed to hear. So thanks."

For a few beats, she didn't reply. And then she turned to lean next to me, tilted her beer bottle toward mine and clinked the necks. "You're welcome."

We stood that way for the better part of the next hour, until someone came out to find us. I didn't remember who it was, but I did know that time was the closest I got to peace that day.

And now I was sitting in Emmy Carter's driveway, watching as she climbed out of her aging red mini-van and walked to her front door. What the hell was I doing?

She glanced back at me, lights from the small front porch glinting on her red hair. A surge of want filled me, just as it had earlier as I'd watched her move around the bar. I'd always liked Emmy, but something was different tonight. I wasn't sure whether she'd been smiling more, or whether I was suddenly more aware. Whatever, it was why I'd done something I'd never expected and asked Emmy if I could go home with her. It was why I was opening the door of my Jeep now and climbing out, moving steadily toward the house.

She met me at the front door, tossing a quick smile over her shoulder. "So you made it. Didn't lose me in all that traffic?" The teasing in her tone ignited a spark that made me want to wrap my arms around her again, shove her up against the door right here in the dim glow of her porch.

I held back with more restraint than I'd given myself credit for having. "It was touch and go." I jerked my chin toward her van. "Lucky you drive a red vehicle. That thing's hard to miss."

Emmy pushed the door open and moved into her house, laughing. "Good old Red. I know the color's obnoxious, but she runs well, and she's never let us down." She turned around, tilting her head at me. "Are you going to come in, or did you drive all this way just to walk me to my door?"

Smirking, I stepped over the threshold. "Emmy, I'm not that much of a gentleman."

We stood just inside her tiny living room. It was neat without being fussy; the furniture was worn, but it was clean. A colorful braided rug lay in the middle of the gleaming wood floor.

She spread out her hands. "It's not much, but it's home. And it's mine." Her mouth firmed, and she set her jaw. Yeah, a fair amount of pride there, and well-earned, I knew. When Eddy took off for bigger waves, he didn't leave much in the way of support. Emmy had managed to hold onto this house and keep her kids fed and clothed without taking any help, even though I knew it was offered. I remembered Matt saying in exasperation that he hoped Emmy Carter didn't starve on her pride. We'd never have let that happen, of course. But she'd scrapped her way through a shitty time, and she deserved to be proud of what she'd done.

"It's . . . warm." That was exactly right, I decided. "It feels like home. Like you could sit down and have a beer, be comfortable. You can feel the love." I lifted one shoulder. "Sounds corny, but it's true."

She smiled, and her eyes lit with it. "That's the biggest compliment you could give me. My furniture is almost all hand-me-downs, and this place could use a few updates, for sure. But we like it." She hooked her handbag over the top of a ladderback chair and turned toward the arched doorway that looked as though it led into the kitchen. "Want something to drink? I'm having a glass of wine. That's my routine after work on weekends."

I followed. "Sure. Wine sounds good."

"It's better than just good. Jude and I worked this out as part of my salary." She reached to the far side of the refrigerator to a small cabinet. "Daniel made me try it one night, and I just fell in love. But it's way beyond my budget—I'm lucky to be able to swing a bottle of white at the grocery store. So Jude started giving me a bottle every other month or so and calling it a bonus for good work." Emmy uncorked it and took down two glasses from a shelf. I watched in silence as she gave us each a healthy serving.

Handing me a glass, she lifted her own goblet and raised her eyebrows, waiting for me to make the toast.

"To friends." I touched the rim of my glass to hers. "And . . . to whatever comes next."

She held my eyes for a moment and then sipped her wine, closing her eyes and making a humming sound that ran right through me, making my cock sit up and take notice.

"Have a seat." Emmy nudged out one of the kitchen table

chairs with her foot. "Unless you'd rather hang out in the living room."

"No, this is fine." I scraped the chair over the tile and sat down. Emmy did the same across the table. She leaned back, sighing and rotating her neck. I watched as she arched, stretching her back, pulling her green T-shirt tight over her breasts. Clearing my throat, I glanced away. "Was it a long night?"

"I've had longer. And we're not in season yet, so it was mostly local people, which is always nicer for me. Not that I don't like meeting new people—I do. But not when they're like the jerk tonight."

My lip curled, thinking about the dick who'd been harassing Emmy when I got there. "Do you get a lot of that?" It crossed my mind that maybe Jude needed to hire a bouncer for weekends. It wasn't fair to expect Emmy to handle security while she was running everything else.

"Nah." Emmy leaned her elbows on the table, both hands cradling the goblet. "Most of them are pretty chill. We get some college kids who trickle down from Daytona, but they're fun. Other than that, it's families or older couples. Every now and then, someone gets rowdy, but I can handle it. Usually there's someone around to lend a hand if not." She smiled, set her glass down on the table and reached one hand across to touch my arm. "Like you were tonight."

"Yeah, you had that handled. But it was a good excuse for me to get snarly with someone. I need to do that every few days, or I implode. So thanks for letting me bleed some of the mean out."

She rolled her eyes. "Cooper, you're not mean. You're just . . . intense. You're an artist."

I laughed. "Yeah, that's my excuse. My mom used to say I didn't play well with others. Still don't."

"It's not like you're a loner. You have friends. You're not a recluse."

"No, but only because those friends have to put up with me. We've known each other too long. And they don't let me hide away very often."

Emmy bit the side of her lip, reminding me how soft and pliant that mouth had been under mine back at the bar. "You came out tonight without any of them forcing you. At least I'd assume you did. I didn't see any of the posse dragging you into the Tide."

"No." I tried to remember what had made me decide to head out tonight. "Sometimes I get tired of my own shit company." I studied her across the table, taking in the whole enticing package that was Emmaline Carter. Her dark red hair, thick and wavy, was pulled up into a ponytail, but more than one strand had escaped and was curling down her neck. Huge hazel eyes, rimmed with dark lashes, watched me with something more than interest. She was still worrying the side of her lip between her teeth, and it was all I could do not to reach over, lift up her arms and kiss her hard, until she couldn't breathe.

The slim column of her neck led to the scoop neck of her T-shirt above a rack that was just my style. Not huge, but perfectly shaped, so that I could almost feel them in my hands.

I clenched my fists to keep from jumping the gun. There were a few things I had to clear up before we made this leap: my standard waivers and disclaimers.

"Emmy, I know I asked you if I could come home with you tonight, and I'm happy you said yes. But I just want to be clear—"

"Cooper." She hadn't moved her hand from my arm, and now her fingers gripped my wrist. "If this is your warning about how tonight doesn't mean anything, it's just going to be sex, no strings attached—save it. You don't have to tell me how it is. Preaching to the choir, buddy." She leaned back again, casting her eyes up to the ceiling. "My life is full and complicated. Between trying to deal with the kids, keeping us all afloat with the pies and my hours at the Tide, I don't have time to take a bubble bath, let alone try to make a relationship work. I promise, I'm not looking for long-term. Hell, I'm not looking for short-term. I'm just after a good time tonight."

My mouth may have dropped open a little. *Wow.* Emmy had just become my dream girl. "It's not that I don't like you, Emmy, or that I don't think you'd be a great girlfriend. But I don't have it in me for anything more than a night or two, now and then. I've tried it, twice, and I suck at commitment."

"I don't feel insulted at all, Coop. Seriously." She cocked her head, and a teasing smile curved her pretty lips. "I'm going to come clean about something I never thought I'd tell anyone, least of all you. I had a huge crush on you in high school. Like, massive. I used to daydream about the day you'd see me and realize we were meant to be together. And I used to fantasize that you'd hold me, the way you did tonight at the Tide, and kiss me . . . and more." She laughed a little, shaking her head. "The crush went away, and I'm not jonesing anymore for you to decide I'm your one-and-only, but damn, Cooper. I'd be lying if I said I'm not up for making some of those teenaged fantasies a reality tonight."

I stood up and moved slowly around the table between us. Dropping to my haunches next to Emmy's chair, I dragged it around so that she faced me, her legs between mine, and laid my hands on her jeans-clad thighs. Her muscles jumped at my touch, and I pushed my advantage a little, flexing my fingers.

"So tell me, Emmy." I drew small circles with both my thumbs. "What kind of teenaged fantasies did you have about me? About us?"

That flawless pale skin flushed a pretty shade of pink, but judging by the bold gleam in her eyes, it was more interest than embarrassment. "Well, I was pretty young and innocent back in those days, remember. So there was a lot of kissing and being swept into your arms. Maybe some sweaty make-out sessions in the backseat of your car. But I'm happy to say I've come a long way since then."

She leaned forward, sliding her hands up my arms until they rested on my shoulders. For a moment, she looked into my eyes as though trying to decide what to do first. She cupped my face in her fingers and closed the distance between us, capturing my mouth.

Just as it had back at the Tide, the first touch of her lips to mine sent a zing of burning need through my body. I had to fight the urge to knock her out of the chair and onto the tile floor. My hands traveled up over her hips to rest on her waist where it dipped, and I dug in my fingers.

There was no doubt that Emmy wanted this as much as I did. Somehow that only made me hotter, and my cock grew, pressing against the zipper of my jeans. Her mouth was open, her tongue delving to find mine and wrap around it, while her hands stroked my jaw. I tightened my grip on her middle and urged her forward on the chair until her legs had to spread. She wrapped them around me, never breaking our kiss, and I couldn't wait any longer.

I ran my hands down to the tempting little ass that had been making me crazy all night at the bar, watching her bend and shimmy. Emmy lifted enough that I could slip under her, and I lifted her at the same time that I stood.

She tore her lips from mine just long enough to breathe the words into my ear.

"Bedroom. Down the hall, last room on the right."

And then she was on me again, as if that brief break had cost her something precious. I stumbled out of the kitchen toward the dark hallway just beyond. There was just enough light from the kitchen to illuminate the first turn, but then I was on my own. I freed one hand to feel along the wall, distractedly counting doors.

"Here." Emmy reached back and pushed at the wall behind her, which apparently was a door that opened to reveal a small bedroom.

There was sufficient moonlight shining through the open blinds that I could make out the furniture. The bed was a double, neatly made, and I managed to narrowly avoid bumping us into a large oak dresser. The furniture-artisan part of my brain noted that none of the pieces matched. And then I was laying Emmy onto the mattress, and I didn't care what any of the furniture looked like.

With her hands free, she grasped the bottom of my shirt and pulled it up, trapping my arms and head until I lent a hand, tossing it away. Her gaze wandered down my chest, and she smiled almost wolfishly as her eyes half-closed.

"God, you're gorgeous, Cooper." Her fingers traced down the center of my pecs to skim over my abs, and I shivered.

Emmy laughed softly. She raised her head, touching her lips to a spot just below my nipple, brushing a kiss there before her tongue darted out to lick.

"And you taste damned sinful, too." She spoke against my heated skin and moved her mouth higher to cover the flat disc. I groaned when her teeth nipped.

"Scoot up some." I urged her toward the center of the bed, and she acquiesced, sitting up a little to slid her backside. I took advantage of her position to strip off her shirt and throw it over my shoulder. The bra she wore beneath the tee was a simple cream-colored cotton, nothing particularly sexy, but on her, with her tits spilling out over the top, it was damned erotic. I mimicked her move and traced the slope of one breast before letting my mouth follow its path.

"I didn't expect anyone else to see my underwear tonight." Emmy propped herself on her elbows, a position that thrust her boobs forward even more. I licked my lips and tried to pay attention to what she was saying. "So I'm sorry it's so . . . normal. Boring."

"There's not the least thing boring about you or your body, Em." I palmed both of her breasts and let my thumb circle the shadows of her nipples beneath the material. "You're beautiful."

She smiled but shook her head. "Thanks, but I don't harbor any illusions about how I look. I've had three kids and I'm getting closer to forty every day. I don't have time or money to spend hours in a gym, and if I were to lay out on the beach, I'd fry instead of tanning." One slim shoulder lifted. "But this is me."

The way she spoke reminded of how she'd described her house. I frowned. "Emmy, I don't want to argue with you, but trust me. I don't sugarcoat shit. If I didn't think you were fucking sexy, I wouldn't say you are. I just wouldn't say anything at all." I bent my head over one tit and sucked the stiff peak into my mouth, cotton bra and all. Emmy hissed in a breath.

"Okay, I guess I have to believe you." She was breathless, and knowing I'd made her that way made me smile again. "I don't want you taking your mouth off me long enough to argue."

I moved my head to her other boob, pausing between them just long enough to whisper to her. "I may be an artist with wood, but seeing you . . . it makes me wish I had the talent to paint. I'd do your portrait just like this, with the moonlight spilling over your alabaster skin. Only you'd be completely nude."

"That can be arranged." Her words ended abruptly when I sank my teeth into her other nipple. I felt her watching me and opened my eyes.

"Lean up. Let me take this off." I insinuated my fingers under her back, reaching for the hook to her bra. "I want you naked under me. And I can't wait anymore." I reached the clasp and twisted until it sprang loose. While she slid the straps off her arms, I shifted my attention to the button of her jeans. Emmy sucked in her stomach when the back of my fingers touched her just above the waistband.

"Do you want me to do that?" She half-sat again, her eyes on my hand.

"Absolutely not. This is part of my fun." I finally got the button undone and eased down the zipper, revealing a pair of brightly flowered bikinis. I ran my index finger just under the elastic. "Festive."

"Oh, God, I'm wearing the flowers." She let her head drop back, laughing. "I forgot. I was in a hurry after I dropped the kids with my parents, and I just got a quick shower and pulled out the first pair I found."

"I like them. Wasn't there some book about a woman's, um garden?"

She laughed even harder. "I can't believe you brought that up. Yes, okay, so I have flowers covering up my lady garden. Go ahead and enjoy the irony."

"I'd rather enjoy your lady garden." I tugged on her jeans and she lifted her hips. As they dropped to the floor, I resettled myself between her legs, my face at the juncture of her thighs. Pressing small quick kisses over the cotton of her underwear, I teased the soft skin just below the edge. "Do you have any issues with multiple orgasms?"

"God, no." She pushed herself up a little further to see

me. "But I have to warn you . . . it's been a long time. I might not take—oh, my God."

Her voice trailed off on a long moan when I slipped one finger inside her panties to explore her wet folds. She dropped back flat on the mattress, and her hands, near her hips, clutched at the comforter.

I teased her a minute with my finger before I couldn't deal with the underwear in my way anymore. With a muttered curse, I pulled it off her, not caring where it landed. Holding her legs apart, I dropped my mouth to her waiting pussy.

My lips covered her, and I licked once in a long, slow stroke before zeroing in on the small button of nerves that clearly needed the most attention. The moment my tongue touched her there, Emmy arched her back, crying out words I couldn't understand. I slid two fingers inside her, curling to find the spot that would make her insane. I must've hit it right away, because she went stiff and still, her mouth partly open and her eyes screwed shut. I pumped my hand against her and kept my mouth moving until she sagged back onto the bed and moved her hand to push sluggishly at my head.

Her skin had flushed a beautiful pink, and her body was lax and lazy. I didn't think I'd ever seen a more enticing, erotic sight as Emmy just after she'd come.

Kissing up her stomach, pausing to touch my tongue to the underside of her breast, I lay alongside her, my hand skimming lightly over her arm. She turned her head, and her eyes flashed open to meet mine.

"Holy fuck, Cooper." She almost slurred the words, as though she'd had a little too much wine. "Holy freaking fuck."

"I take it that's good?" I leveraged myself up on one elbow and kissed her lips, this time with a lazy softness.

"Good isn't even in the same universe. It was . . . beyond even my grown-up fantasies. But fifteen year-old Emmy is shocked out of her mind."

I laughed, teasing one of her nipples with the very tip of my finger. "Glad I could accommodate both of you."

She rolled onto her side, laying her hand on my cheek. "Well, it was a beginning. After all, I'm pretty sure someone mentioned multiple orgasms." She pressed her mouth to my chest as her hand dropped the button of my jeans. "And you have on way too much clothing. You're making me self-conscious."

"We can fix that." I began to help her, only to have my hand batted away.

"Hey, hey, no taking my fun away. As a matter of fact, there's something I always wanted to try. You game?"

"Baby, no man alive would ever say no to those words, when the woman speaking them is naked and has her hand near his dick."

"Then lay back and let me do my thing." She shimmied down my body, pressing her tits to my chest and making me groan. It was my turn to lean up and watch as she brought her mouth to the button and took it into her mouth, working to undo it with her teeth and tongue.

On paper, I never would've thought having a woman undo my jeans with only her mouth would be sensual. But Emmy's chin rubbed over my zipper as she worked, and once she had the button free, she caught the zipper tab in her teeth and tugged it down . . . with frustrating and mind-blowing slowness, all the while her hot breath blew on the part of my body that felt like it just might explode at any moment.

When she'd unzipped the jeans, Emmy hovered for a second before she brought her mouth back down to cover me over the cloth of my boxers. She licked the ridge of my cock until the material was soaked. And then she sat up and slapped at my ass.

"Lift up so I can get these off. I want you naked and writhing under me." She said it with so much anticipation that I couldn't move fast enough to get the damned pants off me, tossing away the boxers at the same time.

Once they were gone, she didn't waste any time, and I lifted up a silent prayer of thanks for that fact. She held my erection at the base with one hand, fisting the other around me and moving it up and down with the perfect amount of pressure. I closed my eyes and breathed out, concentrating on holding myself in check. So intent was my focus that when her lips closed over the head of my cock, it took me utterly by surprise.

I'd had my share of blow jobs in my life. Hell, I'd had my share and probably ten other guys' shares, too. But mostly I'd found the women who gave them either weren't really into it, only doing it because they thought it'd give them some kind of leverage with me, or because someone had convinced them that real women had to give head during every sexual encounter. Both reasons left me cold and a little bored.

But Emmy was completely different. She looked at me like I was the dessert she'd been denying herself for way too long.

And when she sucked me further into her hot, tight mouth, her hum of pleasure vibrated throughout my body, making me jerk involuntarily and thrust myself further in.

To her credit, she didn't gag or lose her rhythm. Her tongue swirled around my shaft, and her teeth scraped just enough to tantalize. When she sucked in her cheeks and pulled up, almost but not quite releasing me, I felt the familiar tingle that warned I was about to lose control.

"Emmy . . . baby. God, that feels incredible, but I'm close. I don't want to come in your mouth. Not this time. I want to be inside you, feel you coming with me."

She didn't answer, but she lifted her mouth from my cock, laying her head on my stomach and looking up at me. "Are you sure? We can do that next time. We have all night." That pink tinge returned to her face. "I mean, I do. Not that I expect—you can, of course, but don't feel like you have to."

"Emmy." I rubbed her cheek with the backs of my fingers. "Stop. You're not pressuring me. I plan to spend the night making you come. I just want the first time I come to be both of us, together. With me buried deep inside you, looking into your eyes and you staring up at me. I want to see you fall apart, with my name on your lips and your skin with that beautiful blush that spreads down, across your throat and to the tops of your tits."

Her mouth curved into a smile. "I think I can get behind that kind of thinking." She turned her face against me, touching her lips to my stomach and then working her way back up to my chest and then to my chin. I rolled both of us over so that I leaned over her again, lowering my head to capture one rosy nipple in my mouth.

Her fingers caressed the back of my neck, playing with the short hair there, pressing me closer to her. I slid to lavish the same attention on her other breast, leaving my fingers to tease the peak my lips had left behind before I walked them down, down lower. Delving into her core, I pressed my thumb to her clit.

"Cooper, please . . ." It was nearly a moan.

"Please what?" I murmured into her ear. "Tell me, Emmy. What do you want?"

"You, inside me. Now, like right fucking now."

I grinned. Emmy Carter had a dirty mouth during sex. Who'd have guessed it? "Do you like it hard, Emmy? Hard and fast? Or soft and slow?"

She gasped, arching against my hand as I plunged two fingers into her slippery channel. "I don't care right now, as long as your cock is inside me." She ended on an almost-sob, and I knew she was close to losing control. I wanted to be deep inside her when that happened.

"Okay, baby. Do you have a condom here?"

She groaned and swore. "Fuck! No, I don't have anything. It's been—there's been no one—damn it, no. I'm sorry."

"It's all right, I've got one in my wallet. I just thought if you had one closer—hold on a minute." It almost killed me to stop touching her as I dropped from the bed to the floor and fumbled for my jeans. First, of course, I found Emmy's and didn't realize it until the back pocket was empty. When I finally got my hands on my wallet, they were nearly shaking. I managed to pinch out the rubber, rip open the wrapper and roll it on, all while climbing back up onto the mattress.

"Are you ready, Em?" I settled between her legs, my dick straining toward her.

"God in heaven, so ready." Emmy grabbed my ass and urged me forward, but I didn't need the invitation. I found her entrance and thrust into her body in one long, hard movement.

For the space of several heartbeats, neither of us moved. Emmy was whispering something low, but I was just still, in rapt awareness. Her hands roamed up my back, a light touch that gave me goosebumps. I ground against her, and she caught her breath.

"Yes, do that again." Her eyes closed and her forehead knit together, as though she was trying to find something she'd lost. When I repeated that same move, everything smoothed out and she bit down on her lip.

"No, baby, don't try to be quiet." I bent my head to capture her lips, swiping my tongue into her mouth and consuming her breath. "Give it to me. Give it all to me."

"I was wrong, I do care. Not slow, not now. Fast, and hard. Fuck me, Cooper. Hold me down and use me. I want to come around your cock, and I want you to eat me alive—"

Whatever she was going to say next was lost when I fastened my lips onto hers again at the same time that I plunged into her, hard and fast. I didn't stop, and God, it felt good. It felt like I was flying, lifting up above the earth, and I'd never felt like this. My balls tightened, and I knew I was close to the edge.

"I'm about to come. Emmy, are you close?"

She wrapped her legs around me, her heels digging into

my ass, spurring me on, bucking her hips to meet my thrusts. She didn't answer in words, but I felt the beginning of her climax when her inner walls began to tighten around me. It was all I needed: with one last hard plunge, an obscene wave of pleasure took me under, almost drowning me in its wake. I came hard and long, my gaze on Emmy's wide hazel eyes, watching her ride the same inescapable current.

When I could breath again, I shifted to the side, so as not to crush her. Emmy laid one hand on my arm, rubbing up and down as though to assure herself I was real. And here.

"So, how does high school Emmy feel now?" I brushed a strand of hair out of her face, catching the smile that curled her lips.

"That Emmy is thinking she should've held out for you all those years ago. Should've waited and tried harder to get you to notice her. Because damn, she never had anything like that."

I chuckled. "And how about grown-up Emmy? How's she feeling?" It was crazy to need this kind of assurance, I knew, but it mattered. *She* mattered. This might be just a one-time deal, but it was still Emmy, and I wanted tonight to be incredible for her.

"Grown-up Emmy is in full agreement with her former self. She thinks she's been missing something all these years, too." She paused a minute before adding, "And she also thinks she needs to invest in condoms for her nightstand drawer."

"Sorry about that. I should've thought beforehand, but I kind of got caught up." I picked up her hand, lifting the knuckles to my lips.

"No, not your fault. Most women probably are better prepared, but most women probably have a need to be better prepared." She bit the side of her lip again, and her cheeks went pink, as though she'd said more than she'd planned.

"If you're trying to tell me you don't usually bring men home from the bar, Emmy, don't. I don't think that. We live in a very small town, and if you were regularly luring unsuspecting males into your bed on weekends, word would get around. I know you respect Jude and your job too much to do that."

Emmy lifted her shoulder in a half-shrug. "I hope that's why I don't do it, but the truth might be that bringing a guy home could cost me too much time and energy, neither of which I have in abundance. It's just plain too much trouble."

"Then why did you say yes to me?" I twined our fingers together and rested our joined hands on my chest, just above my heart.

She blew out a long sigh. "I told you, I had that crush. And then . . . I don't know. I guess maybe because you asked. And you're Cooper. I know you. Maybe, too . . . I've been lonely. I always say I don't have time to feel alone, but sometimes you just want a human connection, you know? I love my kids, and my parents would do anything for me. I have friends. But sometimes you just want someone to *see* you. To really care, and pay attention. You're always like that, Coop. You have the gift of listening, and making the other person feel like she's the most important girl in the world. I guess I needed that tonight."

I understood, more than she could know. I drew her closer to me, so that her head lay on my chest, her face close to our linked hands. "Thank you for saying yes, Em. I needed that connection tonight, too. I know what you mean about feeling alone. I hope that even after tonight, if you need to feel that again, you'll come to me." I smoothed back her hair, running my fingers through its thick length. "When I look at you, Emmaline Graham Carter, I see a beautiful woman who's been strong for a very long time. Who's made it on her own against some pretty fucking incredible odds, but who hasn't let those things make her hard. I see a good friend, a soft heart and a wicked sense of humor." Pressing my lips just above her ear, I added, "And I see a woman who's passionate. Sexy. Brave. You own it, Em. That's a huge turn-on, that confidence."

She laughed, shaking against me. "Oh, Cooper. That part's just bravado. If you really knew . . ." She trailed off, and I knew without looking that she was probably blushing again.

"If I really knew what?" I held her closer, tracing tiny circles on her upper arm with my forefinger.

She took a deep breath. "You're only the second man I've ever been with. Had sex with."

I frowned, trying to make sense of what she'd said. "The second—you mean just—"

Emmy nodded, her hair tickling my chest. "Yup. That's right. Eddy and you. Pathetic, isn't it?"

"No, it's not—wait, you didn't have another boyfriend in high school?"

"Just Eddy. We started dating when we were sophomores."

"And since he left?"

She shook her head again. "No one. At first I was too busy, too worried all the time. And then by the time I could sort of breathe again, men weren't exactly knocking down my door. Not when I have three kids."

I was in awe. "How long has Eddy been gone?"

Her voice was muffled against my chest. "Just over three years."

"Christ Jesus, Em." I tried not to sound shocked, but *damn.* "Wow. How do you do it? I can't imagine living that long without sex."

She giggled. "I'm a woman. I have needs, yes, but they fall somewhere behind kids, keeping food on the table and not losing my house. So . . . yeah. I take care of myself when I can. When I'm not falling asleep. Otherwise, I just hope nothing gets too rusty before I get the chance to use it again."

I tipped her chin up until she met my eyes. "Emmy, I have to tell you three things. First, those needs are important. Second, nothing, not one part of you, was rusty. Third . . ." I rolled over until she was beneath me again, caged by my arms. "I'm making it my personal mission to make up for all your lost time tonight. So I hope you don't have any plans for tomorrow until it's time for you to go to work, because you're going to need a long nap to make up for missed sleep."

Her eyes got big, and her smile was bright. "Who am I to get in the way of a mission?"

Chapter Three

Emmy

ONE OF THE FIRST THINGS I'd learned when Eddy hit the skids, as my mother put it, was that single moms don't get a day of rest. There is no such thing as a day off. No holidays, no girls' nights out. I was on the clock twenty-four/seven.

So when I started working at the Tide and my parents suggested that it would just be easier for them to take the kids all weekend long, rather than traipse back and forth from my house to theirs, I decided to say yes fast. I also decided that I'd never set an alarm for Saturday mornings. Instead, I let the sun wake me and got up when I was ready. It was my only real indulgence.

On that Saturday morning, I smiled when I felt the warmth of sunlight hit my face and begin to rouse me. *I must've slept really well last night. I can't remember when I've felt so relaxed.*

I stretched out one arm and froze when it hit a solid form. A solid masculine form. A solid naked masculine form.

As images from the night before flooded my mind, I burrowed into my pillow. *Cooper. I'd slept with Cooper. Shit, I did a hell of a lot more than sleep with him.*

Cooper had more than accomplished his mission to help me make up for the last three years. I'd lost count of how many times I'd come, against his mouth, against his hand, with his cock pounding deep into me . . . even thinking of it now gave me a little throb between my legs. I sighed and turned my head, not able to resist sneaking a peak at him.

His back was toward me, and I lay for a few minutes, just taking in the sight of his muscles and tanned skin. He had both arms wrapped around his pillow, as though he were afraid I'd try to take it from him. Holding back from running my fingers over his roped shoulders and forearms was killing me. There was definitely something about a man's arms . . . I liked a nice tight ass, and a broad chest made me melt, but powerful arms tempted me to just lick them up and down.

I swallowed a sigh and gave myself a stern if silent lecture about playing it cool on the morning after a hookup. I needed to be breezy. Yes, that was the right word. Not unfriendly, not cool; Cooper should know how much I appreciated and enjoyed last night, but I had to convey this without sounding clingy or pathetically grateful. I wasn't that kid anymore who wanted to faint whenever Cooper Davis was near, and I had to act like a grownup.

My first challenge as a breezy grownup was to get out of bed without letting him see me naked. I knew it was silly, since he'd seen all of me and then some last night, but it'd been mostly dark, and moonlight was definitely a friend to the over-thirty woman. This morning my bedroom was flooded with bright and unadulterated sunlight, a harsh glare that wasn't going to do me any favors. If I moved stealthily—and right now, before he was awake—I could get to my closet. I tried to remember if I'd left anything in there I could toss on fast, since most of my shorts and T-shirts were in the dresser on the other side of the room. The side of the room Cooper was facing now with his sleeping eyes. The side of the room that also held the door, which led to the bathroom, where my robe was hanging on a hook.

It was a dilemma, and one I wasn't certain how to tackle. I might be able to slide off the bed without waking him up, but I was pretty sure the only things in my closet were shoes and dresses. Greeting Cooper dressed in the long pink monstrosity I'd worn in my cousin Lydia's wedding five years ago might be worse than letting him see me naked in the daylight.

"Are you staring at me?" His voice, muffled by the pillow, made me jump. "It feels like you are. And that's a little creepy, being watched while I sleep."

"I'm not staring at you." Well, I wasn't. Not at this moment, anyway. "I'm staring at the door."

"Oh, well, that makes more sense. Why're you staring at the door? Are you expecting someone?"

I gave his leg a half-hearted kick. "No." I paused before I decided to come clean. After last night, I really didn't have any secrets. "I was trying to figure out if I could get to my robe without waking you up."

"And where is your robe?"

"Hanging in the bathroom."

"And why do you need it, exactly?"

"Because I'm naked."

"And that's a problem . . . why?"

I smiled, warm gladness filling me. I liked that he didn't view my nudity as a problem but rather as something to enjoy. I still didn't want him to see me without clothes in the light of day, but it was sweet that he wanted that.

"Because I'm not comfortable with you seeing me naked. In the daytime. I mean, it's so bright."

"Uh-huh." He rolled over, the sheets rippling around his body like water sluicing around a dolphin. Settling to face me, he opened one eye. "Em, you know, sometimes people *are* naked in the daytime. Sometimes they even have sex in the day. Novel concept, huh? Ever hear of afternoon delight?"

"It's not afternoon, and yes, you dweeb, I know people are naked and screwing during the day. But that doesn't change how I feel." I drew in a long breath. "What you said about my body last night was wonderful, Coop. But I'm not a nubile nineteen-year old. I don't want you to watch my ass while I prance around the room."

"Oh, you're going to prance? Well, hell. That does change things." Cooper shifted to his back, rolling the pillow into a bolster as he sat up and leaned against the headboard. "This I'm definitely going to watch." The top of the sheet just barely came to his hips, and it did nothing to disguise his morning wood.

I shook my head and rolled my eyes. "Come on, Cooper.

Be a sport. Close your eyes or cover them, whatever, while I run out and put on my robe."

He rubbed at the side of his neck. "What'll you do to reward me if I say yes?"

I tilted my head. "What do you want?"

A slow smile spread over his lips. "I want you to straddle my lap, right now, and ride me."

Oh. My. God. Desire tingled down my spine, ending in my core. I ran my tongue over my bottom lip, aware of Cooper's watchful gaze. "If I do that, it'll defeat the purpose. You'll see me naked anyway. So why would I reward you by giving you something you're supposed to be not doing in order to get the prize?"

His forehead wrinkled. "Huh? Did you even understand what you just said?"

"Not really, but it doesn't matter. You know what I mean."

He considered, his finger absently brushing against his upper lip, making me want to run my tongue over it. "But if it's your ass you're worrying about me seeing, I won't. Just your front. So see, it's a win-win. You get something you want, I get something I want." He rolled a little toward me, just enough to cup my breast. "And I really, really want, Emmy."

So did I. I kept still for a minute. "Didn't you get enough last night?" It wasn't meant to sound like a complaint, and luckily Cooper didn't take it that way. He laughed a little as his thumb circled my already-stiff nipple.

"Did you?"

I knew I should answer yes. Being breezy definitely didn't include a morning quickie. But his lips parted that moment, and his fingers rolled my nipple, making me catch my breath.

"No."

Before the syllable had even left my lips, Cooper lifted me up and over, onto his body. I struggled to untangle my leg from the blanket and settle on him, all the while working to hold the sheet up to my chest.

"Drop the sheet, Emmy. Come on, a deal's a deal. I get the front, you hide the back."

I shook my head, but at the same time, I couldn't help smiling. He was just crazy. But he was right; I'd promised. I let the white cotton sheet flutter from my fingers, exposing my boobs and stomach to his gaze.

If I'd expected to see him try to hide his disgust, I'd have been disappointed. There was nothing in Cooper's eyes as he looked at my body except want and admiration. He raised his hands to lift both of my breasts, squeezing as he raised his head to capture one pink tip.

"Gorgeous, Em. Perfect."

His words, his voice and his eyes, all working in concert, created a swell of intense desire inside me. I couldn't wait another minute, and I leaned forward to find the last condom on the nightstand. Cooper had made a quick and desperate run to his Jeep about three this morning to get the rubbers from his glove box. I didn't want to know why he had condoms there, and I wasn't going to ask. I decided to just be glad he did.

Ripping open the packet, I rolled it down his length, one hand fisted at the base. Cooper groaned, and before he could recover, I lifted myself up and sank down onto his cock.

This morning, there was no lazy, growing need in me. There was only him, his swelling cock inside me, and the impetus to find the exact right way to move that made him hit the spot that drove me mad. I found it and cried out, leaning forward a little to make sure I was in the best position.

"You're so tight. And so wet for me." Cooper spoke through gritted teeth, and I smiled a little, enjoying the power. I was bringing him pleasure, making him feel good. I began to move faster, and Cooper gripped my thighs. Whether he was trying to slow me down or speed me up, I didn't know, but I was close to my own release and kept moving.

Just as everything within me exploded into a million bits of satisfaction, Coop froze, his body tightening in one long muscle. He jerked upwards a few times, rubbing my sensitive flesh and making me cry out again.

I collapsed onto his chest, breathing so hard I wasn't sure I'd ever catch up again. Cooper drew small circles on my back, lulling me nearly back to sleep, before a sharp sting on my ass startled me.

"Okay, woman, I got my reward. Time for me to keep my part of the bargain. Go get your robe, and I'll roll this way and keep my eyes closed. Okay?"

I moaned. "I don't want the robe anymore. Just want to stay here." My lips moved against the skin of his chest, and I felt his goose bumps.

"Let's think this through, logically. If you stay in bed, so will I, because no way in hell am I getting up if there's even the slightest chance *that* might happened again." He skimmed one palm over the globe of my backside. "And if you stay in bed and so do I, pretty soon it'll be time for you to open the Tide. And then Jude will wonder where you are, and she'll panic and call your mom. And your mom will come rushing over here, maybe with your kids, and they'll burst in here, just to find you fucking the very life out of me. And that just sounds like years of therapy bills for your kids."

I was giggling by the time he finished. Pushing on his chest, I sat up a little. "Fine. Since you just carried an idea to its highly unlikely and alarming conclusion, I guess I'll get out of bed and put on my robe." I swung my leg off his body and shoved at his shoulder. "Go ahead now. Turn over and don't open your eyes until I say. Promise?"

"I already did promise." But he slapped one hand over his heart anyway and spoke low. "I promise not to look at your ass while you're getting your robe. Satisfied?"

Grinning more than a little smugly, I paused on the edge of the bed, looking back over Cooper's drool-worthy body. "Oh, yeah. Satisfaction is a given." I jumped up from the bed and dashed into the bathroom.

"There better not be any prancing going on in there!" Cooper yelled to me as I struggled to get my arms in the sleeves. "Not where I can't see!"

I tied the belt securely and went back into the bedroom. "It's safe to open your eyes now. Thanks for being a gentleman."

Cooper turned his head in the pillow so that I could see just one eye. "Thanks for the reward."

"Is it still a reward if I get as much out of it as you do?" I leaned against the door jam, appreciating the view as Cooper rolled again and the sheet slid down his hips.

"Oh, baby, that's even more of a reward." His eyebrows waggled. "Now go away. I need to get up, and I know you want to ogle my ass. I have to hold onto my dignity, you know."

I couldn't hold back my laughter as I headed for the kitchen, leaving Cooper and his dignity alone in my bedroom.

Since I'd never had a hookup, I wasn't sure of the breakfast protocol. But having an overnight guest usually meant providing at least the basics, so I took the plunge and made coffee. As it began to drip, Cooper called from the back of the house.

"Hey, Em, is it okay if I take a shower?"

I rested my hip against the edge of the counter, suddenly fighting off an odd sense of déjà vu. It'd been long years since I'd heard a man's voice coming from my room while I cooked. I'd forgotten how much I liked it, the presence of another adult in the house. Particularly a male one. Particularly *this* male one.

Before I could go too far down that dangerous road, I called back to him. "Sure. Clean towels are in the linen closet just outside the bathroom door. Help yourself to anything else you need."

"Thanks, Emmy." The bathroom door closed—I could always tell which door it was, because it tended to stick a little—and a few minutes later, I heard the shower turn on.

Without really thinking about it, I took the carton of eggs out of the fridge and cracked some into a bowl, whipping them into a froth. My favorite cast iron pan was on the burner where it always sat—I used it too often to bother putting it away—and I dropped a dollop of butter in the middle as it heated. When the pan began to sizzle, I added the egg mix and tilted the pan to distribute it evenly.

My movements were automatic, which was a good thing since my brain was buzzing in too many directions to pay attention. Last night had been . . . I didn't have the right words for what being with Cooper had meant to me. I'd been ignoring crucial parts of myself for too long, and last night, they'd roared to life. It was more than just the sex, although . . . damn. That had been enough by itself. But Cooper had talked to me. Listened to me. He'd complimented me, and I knew his words were sincere, because I'd never known this man to tell a lie, even in the interest of sparing feelings. This morning, I felt like an entirely new person. Instead of dreading the new week, I was invigorated.

Digging a spatula out of the drawer, I flipped the eggs over and added salt and pepper, turning down the heat. While they finished cooking, I opened up the wooden bread box on the counter and unwrapped a loaf of butter wheat bread that I'd made Thursday. There was just enough for four slices, which I laid carefully on the racks in the oven to toast.

A loud thump down the hall told me Cooper had finished his shower. I smiled as I heard him whistling. I hoped that meant he'd enjoyed last night, too. And this morning.

It's a one-time deal, Em. Don't go getting gooey and sentimental. Remember, breezy.

I nodded to myself, repeating the mantra in my head as I took out dishes and plated the eggs. He came into the kitchen just as I opened the oven to check the bread.

"Do I smell eggs? God, I'm never leaving." His easy grin told me he was teasing. "My life is a great tragedy, because I love breakfast. Eggs, bacon, toast, pancakes, waffles, French toast, juice—you name it. Love it. And I can't cook any of it to save my soul."

The bread wasn't ready, and I shut the oven, leaning against the door as I folded my arms across my chest. "You can't learn how to do it?"

Cooper shook his head. "I make do with all the other meals. I can manage a chicken and even spaghetti sometimes. But there's something about anything with eggs that just eludes me."

"So what do you do?" I unhooked two mugs from beneath the cabinet and poured coffee. "Or is that why your life is such a tragedy, because you never get breakfast?"

He picked up his coffee and inhaled it, eyes falling shut. "Ah. That's the stuff." Shaking his head when I pointed out the sugar and cream, he took a long drink. "Well, most days I just have coffee and maybe a granola bar. But sometimes I go to that little diner out on route 18."

I raised one eyebrow. "I don't know if you're aware, but one of your very best friends owns a restaurant not five minutes from your house. And she serves a mean breakfast."

"I know." Coop looked miserable. "But if I went to the Tide, I'd have to be sociable. Jude expects me to hold a conversation when I go there. When I go to the diner, no one cares about me. They don't know me from Adam, and they leave me alone.

TAWDRA KANDLE

So sometimes, that's what I do." He took another sip and then looked up at me with serious alarm. "Don't tell Jude, though. I don't want to hurt her feelings."

If I knew anything about my boss, she was fully aware of her friend's extracurricular restaurant activities. Not much escaped Jude, and Crystal Cove was small enough that word got around pretty fast. But I drew an X over my heart and nodded. "Not a word." I peeked into the oven again and turned it off before I opened the door. "Toast is ready." Using my fingers, I picked up the slices fast and dropped them onto our plates. "Oooh! Hot."

"Imagine that, something coming out of the oven is hot." Cooper shook his head. "Why don't you have a toaster? It's this new-fangled device that cooks bread so we don't have to burn off our fingers."

I stuck out my tongue at him. "I don't need a toaster. They only work on faux bread and nasty breakfast pastries. We don't eat them in my house, so we don't need a toaster. The oven works just fine, thanks." I carried the plates to the table and set them down. Cooper took the seat across from me, just as he had last night.

"This looks amazing. But what's faux bread?"

I brought over forks, knives and butter. "Any bread that isn't made at home is faux bread. Any bread that comes in plastic bags is faux bread." I sat down and pointed at the toast on his plate. "That is not faux bread."

He forked off a bite of eggs and laid it on a corner of toast before biting into it. I watched his face, grinning when his expression changed to surprised bliss.

66

"Oh my God, Em. This . . . this is amazing. It's the best bread I've ever tasted. You made this?"

I smiled. "I did. And if you think it's good toasted, you should try it fresh out of the oven. That's when it's best. My kids fight for who gets the first slice."

"I don't blame them. I'd mow them down." He took another bite, swallowing before he went on. "The eggs are great, too. Seriously, Em, thanks. This is a treat."

Breezy. "Well, I had to eat, and so did you. Glad you like it." I turned my attention to my own plate, and we ate in companionable silence for a few minutes.

"What do you usually do on Saturdays?" Cooper pushed away his empty plate and leaned back in his chair, his eyes on me.

I shrugged. "Catch up, mostly. I do paperwork for the pie business, email managers and booking agents about the acts playing at the Tide in the next few weeks. Pay bills. Make lists for the baking I'll be doing."

"So, you pretty much take it easy?" I couldn't miss the teasing note in his voice.

"Yeah, pretty much. My life is so glamorous. Try not to be jealous." I rolled my eyes, one side of my mouth curving into a smile. "How about you? Are Saturdays just another work day?"

"Sometimes." His eyes fastened on the coffee mug, and he used one finger to move it slightly. "When Lex was smaller, I usually spent weekends with her. Or at least most weekends. But now she's in high school, and she's got this thing called a social life. So old Dad gets relegated to the occasional Sunday."

I felt a pang. I was thankful that I didn't have to share my kids with Eddy. He hadn't seen them in person in over two years. "I'm sure it's not that bad. I've seen Lexie with you, remember. She adores you."

He smiled. "We're good. She calls and texts all the time, and I know this is just part of her growing up. Jolie says she never sees her, either. Lex is always running from one thing to another."

I'd met Jolie, Cooper's first ex-wife. She was a pretty brunette with flashing dark eyes. Jude always said Cooper and Jolie got along better as a divorced couple than they ever had when they were married, and I could see that was true. Jolie lived with a banker up in Daytona, and she seemed to have found her peace with life. Lexie was a lovely and well-adjusted young girl. She'd worked for Jude a few summers, and I'd enjoyed getting to know her.

"I don't know what I'm going to do when my kids are that age. Cam's getting close, but boys mature slower. I'm hoping he takes the real slow route."

Cooper nodded. "Still, being in the Cove is the best. They can walk or ride their bikes to just about anything, so they have some freedom without the risk. I loved growing up on the beach, in this town."

"That's true. I did, too." I grinned a little. "I used to ride my bikes to your baseball games. Not that you would've noticed."

He winced. "You're right, unfortunately. Back in those days, I was a jerk. Thought I had the world by the short hairs, being the big baseball player. Getting that scholarship. I had the whole thing planned out, and I didn't have time to pay attention to anyone else."

"You weren't that bad." I felt I had to defend the Cooper Davis who'd won my heart way back then. "You were sweet to me, once."

"Really? When was that?"

I hesitated. For so long, I'd held that story close to me; it was at first an exciting taste of what life might hold, and then it faded into a memory that brought back all the shiny potential of those days.

"It was right before you graduated. I was at the high school for orientation, and I got lost. I ran smack into you, and you helped me find where I needed to go next. You were so nice, and you didn't make me feel stupid. I really appreciated that."

Cooper frowned. "I wish I could say I remembered it. I'm glad I wasn't an asshole to you, but I think that was the exception, not the rule." He regarded me steadily across the table. "Funny to think what if . . ." His voice trailed off, and I wondered if his what-if was anything like mine. What if Cooper had talked to me a little longer? What if he'd seen me at one of his baseball games and remembered me? What if we'd dated, and fallen in love? Would we have been just a quick fling before he left for college, or would we have stuck? Would our lives have been completely different?

I spoke first, breaking the silence. "It was so long ago. I was just a baby, not even a freshman yet. The age difference was pretty vast in those days." I didn't say what I was thinking, that now it didn't matter at all. We were both unattached adults.

Cooper stretched his arms over his head, groaning with the effort. It reminded me of how his muscles tensed when he was in the throes of an orgasm, and I had to close my eyes before I melted into a puddle right there in my chair.

"I better get out of here and let you get on with your exciting Saturday." He stood, pushing in the chair, and picked up his breakfast plate. "I'll help you clean up."

"Don't worry about it." Suddenly, I wanted him to go. If he wasn't going to stay—and he wasn't; he'd been upfront about that, and so had I been. But I needed him to leave so that I could start putting everything back together in my head and adjust to my new life post-hookup.

"I don't mind. You cooked, I should do the washing up."

"Really, Cooper." I took the plate from his hand and carried it to the sink. "I work faster by myself. And I'm sure you've got a lot to do, too. You have a rocking chair to make again, don't you?" It seemed a hundred years ago that he'd told me about his annoying client and the chair that had to be done again. So much had changed in one night.

"Ugh. Don't remind me." He grimaced. "Yeah, I need to figure out how I'm going to juggle everything to make it work." He caught my arm as I tried to pass him, carrying our dishes. "Em, are you . . . you're not mad at me, are you?"

"Mad?" I tried for a laugh and hoped it didn't come out sounding bitter or slightly crazy. "Of course not. Why would I be mad?" There, that sounded breezy, like I couldn't have cared less about him leaving. Like being angry or hurt was the furthest thing from my mind.

"I don't know. When we . . . last night. Before we—when

70

I said about this being a one-time thing. I didn't know." He ran one hand over his short hair, pressing his lips together. "God, I don't know what I'm trying to say. I guess I assumed this was something you did from time to time. Discreetly. I didn't know this was the first sex you were going to have since Eddy."

I put one hand on my hip and looked up at him, my eyes narrowing. "And now that you know you were the first one since my divorce, somehow you feel—what? Responsible for me? Like you owe me something now?"

"No." Cooper shoved his hands into the front pockets of his jeans. "I just—last night wasn't like I thought it would be. I don't want you to think it didn't matter to me."

He was skating perilously close to saying something that I wanted to hear but that I wasn't sure he really meant. I had to stop him before it went too far. "Cooper, we agreed last night was just some benefits between friends. Right? The benefits turned out to be pretty amazing, yeah, but it doesn't change the fact that you're not looking for attachment and neither am I. We don't have time or room in our lives. So let's be grateful for what we did have and move on."

He stepped back, almost as though I'd hit a nerve. I was afraid he was going to argue my point, and God help me, a big part of me wanted him to do just that. I wanted him to tell me I was being stupid and insane, and then pull me back into his arms and down the hall to bed again. But I didn't move or say anything else, and finally he nodded.

"You're right. I just didn't want you to feel—I don't want things to be awkward, Emmy. Your friendship is important to me."

71

Coming from Cooper, this should've meant the world to me. I'd liked Cooper now, as a man, for more years than I'd crushed on him as a kid. But the words felt hollow when they meant friendship was all he wanted.

"Don't worry, Cooper." I forced a smile that I hoped was *breezy*. "Nothing's going to change. I promise I won't start stalking you."

Something flickered in his eyes, but it was gone too fast for me to identify what it was. "Good." He hesitated, as though he wanted to say more, and then turned. "Okay, I guess I better get moving." He leaned down and dropped a kiss on my cheek, almost carelessly. "Thanks again for breakfast, Em. And the shower. And—well. I'll see you around."

"See you, Coop. Have a good day." I stood in the middle of the kitchen, rooted to the ground, as he stalked through the living room. I heard the squeak of the front door and the slam of the screen—the spring was new, and it was still a little tight. After a few more moments, his Jeep started up, and I listened to the hum of the engine as Cooper backed out of the driveway and away from my house.

The house had never seemed so quiet as it did in the wake of Cooper leaving. I turned in a slow circle, suddenly seeing everything through new and different eye. My life, the things I'd managed to hold together, didn't give me a warm happy anymore. Everything felt hollow and empty.

Which was absolutely ridiculous. "Come *on*, Emmy. Grow a pair. You had an excellent night of no-strings hook up sex with the guy you used to lust after. You finally found out what Cooper Davis looks like naked. And it's over, so woman up and get on with it."

The stern pep talk didn't have much effect on me, but I managed to do the dishes and make the bed. I usually pulled off my sheets on Saturday mornings and washed them, but today I couldn't convince myself to get rid of the scent of Cooper that still lingered. I sniffed the pillow, remembering his arms as they held it.

Once the house was in order, I called my mother to check in.

"Good morning, lazy bones!" She half-sang the words with a teasing lilt. "Long night?"

I almost choked on the bottle of water I'd been sipping. *Oh, she had no idea.* "Not too bad. I've been up for a while, but I got sidetracked by chores." True, mostly. Of course, one of those chores had been making breakfast for the man who'd screwed me senseless last night, but she didn't have to know that. "How're the troops?"

"Everyone here is great. Cam and your dad drove out to Aunt Lil's to help put up that new section of fence. They'll be there all day, so the girls and I are working on a few sewing projects and weeding the garden. And then we're making chicken and dumplings for dinner."

"Yum. I hope you're planning to save me some." My mom was the best cook I knew. She'd taught me everything I could do in the kitchen, and she was doing the same with Izzy and Dee.

"Of course. You can have it for lunch tomorrow when you pick up the kids." She paused. "Is everything okay, sweetie? You sound a little off."

"I'm fine." I answered fast, as I always did. Since Eddy had left, I'd made it a practice never to unload on my parents. They didn't need the burden of listening to me whine and bitch, not when they did so much to make my life possible. I didn't tell them about how close I'd come to losing the house back in the beginning. Or how many nights I hadn't slept, because I was up making pies to sell the next day, before I'd gotten the job at the Tide. And the last thing I was going to do was tell my mother about a one-night stand that had left me moping around the house this morning.

"Are you sure?" The woman was both perceptive and persistent. "You know I'm here if you need to talk, honey. About anything."

"I know. Thanks, Mom." I drew in a deep breath and let it out slowly. "Listen, I need to run to the market before it gets any later. I want to get strawberries to put in the scones for the bed and breakfast this week. Can I pick you up anything?"

"Oh, just grab me a pint of strawberries, if you will. Thanks, hon. And don't worry about us, we're doing fine."

I hung up the phone, feeling even lonelier. Hearing about the kids' activities made me happy, because I knew it was good for them to have this time with their grandparents. Cam was very close to my father, and I was glad, because he needed a strong male role model. He certainly wasn't going to find one in his own father.

But as silly as it was, I felt left out, as though life were passing me by while I worked so hard to keep us all afloat. Every week was a constant loop, and I was the one stuck in it. I had a sudden, frightening image of myself, here in the house alone once the kids had grown up and left home. Would I still be baking pies? Working weekend nights at the Tide? Was this how my life was destined to be forever?

Pushing the thought aside, I went into my room to get dressed, trying hard to ignore the flashbacks of the night before and the sneaking fear that maybe that was the last time I was ever going to have sex.

Or at least earth-shattering, brain-exploding sex.

And maybe Cooper Davis had spoiled me for any other kind.

Chapter Four

Cooper

I LOVED MY JOB. IT was more of a way of life than a profession, and sometimes it consumed me, heart and soul. The wood spoke to me, which I knew made me sound like a lunatic, but on some deep level, it was true. When I held the right piece, it sang, and I knew what it was meant to be. What purpose it was meant to serve.

Woodworking was never what I'd intended to do. For as long as I could remember, I'd eaten, slept and breathed baseball. From Little League on up through high school ball, my world revolved around a diamond and nine men on the field of green. I played first base, and I was a decent fielder, but what made me stand out was my hitting. Consistency and strength were the two words I heard most often about myself; my RBI was stellar, and by my sophomore year in high school, I'd broken the homerun record in the county.

Getting the scholarship to North Carolina hadn't been

a surprise. Crystal Cove was a small school, and we didn't get much attention, but when I'd taken our team almost all the way to the state championship two years running, it was pretty much a sure thing that I'd get some kind of deal for college. I had it all planned: I was going to play college ball for three years, unless I was recruited earlier than that. My coaches all expected that I'd be scouted by the majors by junior year at the latest, and then I'd probably leave school and play while I was young. Finishing up my fourth year of college could wait. I had all the time in the world.

Until I didn't. It happened during a game in early spring, when the batter hit one of those shit balls that jumps along the foul line, not quite certain which way it'll roll. I heard the ump call it fair and made a dive to grab it, visions of a double play in my mind. Instead, I hit a patch on the turf and went down, hard. I heard the crack in my arm, up high by my shoulder, and I had a moment to actually think about it—*hell, that's gonna hurt like a motherfucker*—before the pain actually gripped me.

Contrary to what most people in the Cove believed, I didn't lose my scholarship because of the injury. Not directly, anyway. I lost it because I couldn't play ball anymore—or at least, I couldn't play it for now—and I drowned my sorrows in too much booze, too much partying and too little studying. When my advisor called me in to read me the riot act about my grades, I got pissed and quit.

It wasn't a high point of my life.

I returned to the Cove angry. Angry at the college, angry at myself and angry at baseball, the one love of my life

I'd thought would never betray me. My mother, being wiser and more understanding than I ever gave her credit for, left me largely alone, other than assuring me that she was around when I was ready to make decisions. I'd brought my drinking and my party life back home with me. All I needed were my best buds to join me. The posse wouldn't let me down, I knew. These guys had been my friends since elementary school. We didn't have secrets, and we always had each others' backs.

But things had changed over the last few years. Mark Rivers was going to school up in Jacksonville, and he was engaged to a girl he'd met there. Logan was in school, too, closer to home but he still wasn't living in the Cove. Jude and Daniel were getting married in a few months. Matt and Eric were still in town, Matt working at the local surf shop and Eric apprenticing with a plumber. They'd all been glad to see me again, but none of them were interested in being my drinking buddies, which was disappointing. I'd told them as much one night when we all got together down at the beach.

"You're all acting like a bunch of old men. We're still young. Why're we sitting around here when we could be out having fun?"

I'd caught Jude's pained expression as she glanced at Daniel. I hadn't made it a secret that I thought those two were stupid for getting married now, when Daniel was still at school. Jude worked at the Tide, as she always had, and her parents were giving them the tiny apartment above the restaurant after the wedding. Daniel would commute to school come next fall. Their lives were all planned out like mine had been. Only it seemed like theirs might actually work.

Logan stood up from where he was sitting on a driftwood log. "Okay, Cooper. I'll go out with you. Come on, we'll ride up to Daytona."

"Now that sounds like a plan, man." I challenged the rest of them with a look of defiance. "No one else wants to come? Y'all are a bunch of pussies."

Logan gripped me by the arm. "Let's leave now, while you still have friends." He steered me to his truck, which was parked up at the Tide's lot. Neither of us said much as he drove the back roads to Daytona, stopping at a bar I hadn't seen before. It was loud, filled with smoke and rock and roll. Felt like home to me.

Two hours later, I'd nearly gotten in a fight with a biker who outweighed me by at least a hundred pounds. Logan dragged me out of the bar, tossed me into the cab of his truck and drove away, not saying a word. I slumped in the seat.

A few minutes later, he cut the engine, and I looked up, realizing we were just above the beach, looking out over the ocean. The moon was full, and it shone on the dark water, creating the illusion of a pathway from the shoreline to the horizon.

I glanced over at Logan. "Dude, I know everything's changed in the last few years, but I gotta tell you. I'm still not into guys. So I hope you didn't bring me here to make out."

A year ago, Logan would've punched me in the shoulder and called me an idiot son of a bitch. Tonight, though, he just looked at me. "Cooper, when did you get to be an asshole?"

My mouth fell open, and I sputtered, not sure of how to respond. "What the hell, man? We're just shitting around. I didn't—wait, you're *not* into dudes now, are you?" A sneaking horror gripped me—not that I'd care if Logan were gay, but I'd seriously never say a dick thing like that to my friend if he were.

"No, I'm not. But you wouldn't know if I was, because all you've cared about since you got back to the Cove is getting wasted and making all your friends miserable. What's up with that? You know if I hadn't gotten you away from the beach tonight, Daniel was about to deck you. You hurt Jude. All your snide little comments about them getting married—it's making her feel bad. And she's got enough shit to deal with, so lay off, okay?"

I shrugged. "Whatever. I still think they're stupid to get married so young. Why should he tie himself down to her when he could be bagging college chicks? Jude's Cove, all the way. She's never leaving that place, and if Daniel marries her, he won't either."

"Yeah, and leaving the Cove worked out so well for you." Logan's voice dripped with sarcasm. "So what if they end up settling down and staying in the Cove? In case you forgot, that's our hometown, and it's a good place. Stop acting like you're too good for it. Like you're too good for us."

His words hit me in a place that was still tender. Whether it was the booze I'd drunk that night or just that I was finally ready to deal, I curled around my pain, clutching my stomach with one arm and burying my face in the other hand. "Logan. Dude, I fucked up. Big time."

"Yeah." There wasn't any judgment, just acceptance. "You did. But it's done now. What're you going to do next? Keep getting drunk and end up dead or in jail? Or figure out what's going to make it better? What's the new plan?"

We sat for hours, talking. Haltingly at first, I told Logan all about the pain of the arm injury, the devastation of being told that while I could play again, I'd never make it to the Show, the majors.

"That sucks, Coop. Seriously. I'm sorry. You had a gift, man. Watching you play ball was like nothing I've ever seen." He paused. "What else do you like to do?"

I didn't find the path that night, but it was a start. A new start. I spent the next week apologizing to my friends, groveling a lot, and looking for a job. It was a rough time of year, since most of the seasonal jobs had already been filled, but Eric talked to his boss, the plumber, who had a carpenter buddy looking for some help. It didn't pay much, but it would be something temporarily. I applied to the local state college to finish my degree, switching to business instead of liberal arts.

Within a few months, I realized I'd found the answer to Logan's question. I knew what else I liked to do: I liked to work with wood. I stayed with the carpenter until I graduated college, and then I opened my own shop. Logan and Daniel had finished school by then, too, and they were working together, each with his own business. Logan was an architect, and Daniel a contractor.

As the years went on, they formed a new venture together: Holt/Hawthorne Projects. They bought and developed properties, made investments and restored old buildings. I worked with them on almost every job; they'd offered to let me buy into the new company, but I knew myself well enough to decline.

"I don't like people." I was grateful for the offer, but firm in my reasons to say no. "I like to hide out in my workshop. I like to only work for people who don't piss me off. Too much, anyway." By then, I'd married and divorced Jolie, and I'd bought the rundown Cape Cod on the east side of town. Daniel and Logan had helped me turn it into a workshop and showroom, and we'd put in an apartment upstairs. I was well aware of my own limitations. I liked wood more than most people, and if I could do my job without any kind of personal contact, I'd have done it. Unfortunately, that wasn't the case.

I ran my hand over a smooth runner now, examining the piece closely. This was going onto the chair I was remaking for the very pregnant woman and her bitch of a mother. It'd been four weeks since I'd begun the new chair; I only knew that because I'd cut the first wood for the project the morning after . . . Emmy. And it had been two weeks—four long, confusing and frustrating weeks—since I'd laid eyes or anything else on Em.

My night with Emmy wasn't my first one-night hookup. Not by a long shot. Usually I picked up girls from outside the Cove and enjoyed a night of mindless, meaningless sex in a hotel or back at their places. I remembered the dickwad in the bar that night, the guy who'd tried to pick up Emmy when I first got there. The thought that I might have more in common with that jerk than I'd realized made my insides twist.

I never thought about those women I'd slept with after I shut the hotel door behind me. Maybe I chose girls who weren't in the least bit memorable because I needed to forget. Or maybe I forgot them because that was my brain's way of coping with behavior that was really pretty shitty.

But just like I'd known myself well enough not to jump into the joint venture with Daniel and Logan, I also knew that I wasn't cut out for anything more long-term than one night. I'd learned that lesson, not once but twice. And I didn't need to go down for a third time, thanks very much.

I'd met Jolie up in North Carolina, oddly enough. We'd gone out on our first date the weekend before the game that ended my career and changed my life. I'd blown her off in the wake of my injury; she'd called, even come by my hospital room, but I refused to see her. I ran into her at a frat party shortly before I was invited to leave college, and in a fit of drunken sentiment, I told her she was the one who'd gotten away. Whether it was that idea or just that she was wasted, too, we slept together that night. And then I blew her off again.

I'd forgotten all about Jolie once I was back in the Cove. One night a year later, I was at a bar in Daytona with Logan and Eric during spring break. We weren't getting trashed, just having fun by watching the tourists make fools of themselves. I was in a much better place than I'd been before, and it felt good.

"Cooper Davis. As I live and breathe." The voice was familiar, and a tingle ran down my spine.

"Jolie Chapman. What's a nice girl like you . . . well, you know. Hey, Logan, Eric. This is Jolie. We, uh, knew each other up in North Carolina."

She laughed. "Yeah, that's one way of putting it. Nice to meet you, boys. Cooper, dance with me once. I want to make every other girl in this bar jealous."

So we'd danced, and then I went back to her hotel room with her. But this time, I didn't blow her off. I invited her down to the Cove to see where I lived. Introduced her to my family and the posse. After spring break, I took a few weekend trips up to North Carolina to visit her, and one night, I asked her to marry me. To my utter shock, she said yes.

We got married in a little church near her hometown, not far from the college, a month after Jolie graduated. When we went back down to the Cove to live, we both had high hopes. I'd found something I loved to do, and a woman to love while I did it. Jolie was excited to live in a beach town. She had a degree in history, and she wasn't sure what she wanted to do with it yet. But I knew we'd be all right for the time being, even without her working. I was making a little bit of money, and it was easy to live cheap in the Cove.

Jolie tried. We both did. She kept our tiny apartment spotless, cooked delicious food and made friends in town. Jude was sweet to her and tried to include Jolie in whatever she and her friends did, but Jude was also very busy with the Tide and with two babies.

Jolie volunteered at the county history museum and talked about going back to school for her masters, so she could teach history at the state college. But before she could get started, she got pregnant.

We hadn't planned to start a family yet, but I wasn't

unhappy. I figured it couldn't be that hard; Jude and Daniel seemed to have everything under control. But Jolie was devastated. She told me she wasn't sure she'd wanted kids at all, and even if she did, she wasn't ready yet. I had a panicked few days where I was terrified she'd decide to end the pregnancy, and I sighed in silent relief when she said she couldn't do it.

But it was hard on her. The hormonal changes made her moody and weepy and sick. For six months, she could barely keep down any food; it got so bad, she had to be hospitalized for dehydration. For the last three months, she was hot and uncomfortable, and she made sure everyone around her knew it.

When Alexis was born, though, everything changed. I'd been afraid of how Jolie would react to labor and then to the baby herself, but after the nightmare pregnancy, the birth was fast and easy. And when I laid our daughter in her arms, I knew Jolie fell in love as much as I did.

For half a year, things were good again. Lexie was a sweet, good-natured baby, and Jolie was an excellent mother. I was getting more work and spending more time in the workshop, but now that Jolie had the baby to occupy her, I didn't worry about neglecting her so much.

Jolie decided to go back to school when Lex was six months old. She'd found a reliable child care place, and she was determined to make it work. But whether Jolie had changed or I had, or perhaps we were both suffering under the strain of juggling a baby along with my job and her school schedule, things between us got bad fast. We argued all the time. Jolie screamed at me, I yelled at her. She pitched a fit, and I left the apartment, peeling out on two wheels to drive off my mad. It was tense and uncomfortable all the time.

Lexie was eighteen months old when Jolie came to me one day at the workshop. She'd left the baby with my mother, and she'd come to tell me that she was filing for divorce.

"It's ridiculous, Cooper. We're making each other miserable. I don't hate you, and I don't think you hate me, but if I stay, we might end up hating each other. And that is not in the best interest of our daughter. Let's have a happy divorce instead of an unhappy marriage."

Oddly, that's exactly what happened. Once we weren't married anymore, Jolie and I found we could be very good friends. We shared custody without issue, and Lex grew up in two warm homes with parents who respected and liked each other. Jolie met Alton, a financier from Daytona, about five years after our divorce. They eventually moved in together, but they never married. Jolie said she'd decided she just wasn't the type.

As for me, I'd dated here and there, but I didn't get involved with anyone seriously . . . until Karlee. And Karlee cured me for good. We'd met when her grandmother came into the workshop to order a new banister for the historic home she was renovating. The older lady was well-mannered, smart and elegant, and I liked her immediately. Her granddaughter was pretty in an overtly sexy way—big boobs, long blonde hair and legs that went on for days. She was younger than me, but I figured she'd mature and become more like her grandmother. What I hadn't anticipated was that she was certifiably insane.

We'd gotten married on a whim, running down to the is-
lands just the two of us. Within a month, Karlee was accusing
me of cheating on her—I wasn't—and begging me to move
with her to California, where she'd always wanted to live. At
first, I treated her like a spoiled child, firmly telling her no and
waiting for her to understand that word. But as the weeks
went by, I began to realize what a mess I'd gotten into.

She wanted to get pregnant—she loved Lex and wanted
to give her a little sister. And then the next day, she wanted to
audition to pose for a skin magazine. She hated the Cove and
the posse and wanted me to move away. Every day, she greeted
me with a new idea, a new demand. I was quickly worn out.
But the final straw came the day Jude called me from the Tide,
to tell me that she had Lexie there, because Karlee had taken
my daughter to the restaurant and then left without her.

When I apologized to Karlee's grandmother for the ne-
cessity of the divorce, the old woman just shook her head.
"Not your fault, Cooper. We knew she was flighty. We hoped
you'd ground her a bit."

Karlee was my final foray into relationships. After our
divorce, I gave up on girlfriends—and marriage was out of
the question. I had my daughter, whom I adored, an ex-wife
whom I liked, friends who tolerated my anti-social tenden-
cies and loved me anyway, and a career I enjoyed, that kept me
more than comfortable. Asking for more was asking for trouble, and I'd learned the hard way to stay out of trouble.

So no matter how much my night with Emmy Carter
had rocked my world, there was no way it could ever be anything more than just that one night. I had to push aside the

memories of her face as I made her come, and the touch of her hand on my jaw as she kissed me. The sound of her laughter and the image of her sweet little ass in those jeans.

Yeah, those all had to go. So did the dreams I'd been having, where I was in Emmy's bed again. In her body. I'd wake up hard and needing and cursing myself for a fool.

All of this played through my mind as I began to attach the rocker to the chair. It was one of the final pieces; a final sanding, a few coats of paint, and I could put this damn project to rest. I thought about calling the bitch mother and giving her a new pick-up date, but the idea of talking to another human didn't appeal today. I'd call her when I had a firmer idea of timing. God knew if I got held up at all, she'd scream her head off at me, and I had no time for that.

The door to my workshop swung open, but I didn't look up. I didn't have any client meetings scheduled today, so the options for my visitor's identity were limited to a walk-in customer, which was unlikely, given the number of signs in the driveway and yard warning that I saw clients by appointment only. Or it was Lex, who wasn't supposed to be in the Cove today but had been known to persuade her mother to drive her down and surprise me from time to time. Or it was one of the posse, coming by to rattle my cage and shoot the breeze.

When the rocker was secure, I allowed myself one glance up. "Hey, Logan. What's going on?"

"Not much. Just on my way back from a meeting about a new project and thought I might bounce some things off you."

This wasn't unusual. Especially since Daniel had died, Logan often asked for my take on potential investments and new ventures. For one thing, I could weigh in early on how much of my work he'd need and how much it would run him. For another, after working with both of them for so many years, I had a pretty good grasp on some of the contractor details. Logan joked that I could channel Daniel, and in a way, he was right.

"Sure." I jerked my chin in the direction of the upturned crate in the corner. "Pull up a seat and run it by me."

Logan wasn't the least bit put off by the layers of sawdust and woodchips on the floor or even on the crate. He brushed it off and sat down, planting his elbows on his knees as he watched me continue to fine-tune the rocker.

"So you remember the old Riverside Inn? Started out as a regular hotel, and then there used to be a restaurant there about twenty years ago. It's changed hands three or four times that I know about."

I frowned. "On the Osceola River? Yeah, I know it. Hasn't been open in at least ten years."

Logan nodded. "At least. And the last time was with some company that was thinking about making it into a timeshare, before the real estate bubble burst."

"You seriously looking at that?" I shot him a look that was supposed to convey skepticism, but he just grinned.

"Yeah, I am. Or we are. I took Jude canoeing about a month ago, and we were on the Osceola. We went past that old place, and she got all excited. Wanted to look into it, find out the history, all that. The more I looked, the more interested I got. I had an inspector over there last week, and it's structurally sound for the most part."

"Dude, you're talking a shit ton of work. And for what? You want to go into the hotel business?" I shook my head.

"I'm already in the hotel business." Logan leaned forward. "The Hawthorne House is kicking ass. You know Matt always said we needed more places to stay right in the Cove, so we're not sending people all the way out to Elson to find a decent hotel. He was right. We've got a long waiting list at the B and B. A hotel would work here."

I shrugged. "Okay, man. I trust you on the business stuff. You know how to run the numbers and all that." I unwrapped a cotton towel, where I'd been storing the spindles for the rocking chair. "So what do you need from me?"

"I'd like you to go over there with me one day next week and take a look, if you don't mind. But first, I'd like you to come to dinner tomorrow night so we can talk all this over with Jude there. She respects your opinion, and I want to make sure we're going into this with wide open eyes."

Casting my eyes up to the ceiling, I thought for a minute. "Yeah, I can do tomorrow night. Your place or the Tide?" The restaurant was closed on weeknights after five, but sometimes we had after-hours parties or dinner there.

"Our place. Nothing fancy, I'll just toss some steaks on the grill. Jude'll make a salad, and I think we'll have one of Emmy's pies for dessert."

I startled at the mention of her name, dropping two of the spindles onto the floor with a loud clatter. "Fuck!" I reached down to pick up the thin dowels, making sure they hadn't chipped. I didn't see anything, to my relief. That was all I needed, to have to carve out these wood pieces again.

Turning back to Logan, I scowled. "Is Emmy coming to dinner?"

His forehead wrinkled. "No. Why?"

I lifted one shoulder. "You said we were having one of her pies for dessert."

Logan nodded. "Yeah. Jude always buys at least one extra for us to eat at home when she puts in the order for the Tide. Why're you so jumpy? Would it matter if we invited Emmy?"

"Of course not." I returned my attention to the task at hand. "Your house, you do what you want."

"I thought you liked her. Something happen between you guys?"

I almost bobbled the damn spindles again. "What? No. Why? No."

"Did you have a fight or something? She can be a little opinionated, I know. But she's really a nice person."

"No, we didn't have a fight." I decided the best defense was a good offense. "Why in the world would I have a fight with Emmy Carter? What would I even have to talk with her about? Pie crusts? How to serve drinks? The bartenders' code?" Echoes from our flirting that first Saturday night rang in my head.

"What's the bartenders' code?" Logan looked confused, and I couldn't blame him. I was babbling nonsense.

"If you have to ask, you don't need to know it." I paraphrased words I'd heard elsewhere. Seemed like they might apply here. "Anyway, why're we talking about Emmy Carter, anyway?"

"You brought her up." Now Logan was looking at me as if

he truly were afraid I'd lost my mind.

"Yeah, well, whatever. Let's not." I straightened, stretching my back. "So what time for dinner tomorrow night?"

When I told people I was anti-social, it wasn't just talk. As much as I loved my friends, sometimes the idea of spending an evening of small talk, eating party food and drinking frou-frou drinks made me want to shoot myself. I tried to limit how often I said yes to those invitations, no matter who was hosting the party.

But there were a few people who I didn't mind hanging with and a few situations I almost never said no to. Jude and Logan were in that select group; we didn't have to dick around with small talk, because we already knew just about everything about each other, and I saw them enough that there was rarely breaking news to share. Plus, Jude was a damn good cook, and she knew how to feed men: none of these little tiny bites of food, the woman made a mean burger and potatoes.

I pulled my Jeep into the driveway of what I still thought of as Logan's house. He'd designed it and Daniel had built it early in their careers, and Logan had lived there alone for almost twenty years before Jude had moved in a few years back. It'd happened fast in one respect: they'd started seeing each other a little over a year after Daniel died, but once they'd realized how they both felt, Jude was living in Logan's house before they were married that fall.

Of course, on the other hand, Logan had been in love

with Jude since we were all teenagers. He'd never let on, and none of us ever suspected, but after Daniel's death, the two of them together seemed so natural for all of us. Jude's effect on Logan's bachelor pad had been gradual but undeniable, though she was wise enough not to touch the room that was the unofficial headquarters of the posse. The girls called it the man cave or the posse palace. The men just referred to it as the bar at Logan's house. We didn't need to give it a cutesy name; we all knew what it was.

I jumped out of the Jeep and took the steps to the front door two at a time, pausing only to give a cursory knock before turning the doorknob. Up until Jude moved in, I wouldn't have even done that, but I didn't want to walk in on the two of them in the middle of something nasty in the kitchen. And I knew for a fact that wasn't too far-fetched; though none of us tended to kiss and tell when it came to wives and long-time girlfriends, Logan had let slip to me that he and Jude had christened every room of his house, just so that she knew his home was now hers as well.

I'd pretended to gag. "Dude, couldn't you just have written it up in a contract or something? And seriously, this was not something I needed to know. I have to eat there, you know. Gross."

But I was safe today, since as I slammed the front door behind me, I could see through the open great room to the deck, where Logan was manning the grill. Jude had her back to him, leaning over the deck rail that faced the ocean. She was turning her head as though to look at something to her right, but I couldn't see what it was from where I stood.

I went on through the house, calling to them both. "Yo! Logan. Jude. I come bringing wine. I picked up a bottle of that Cab we all liked . . ." My voice trailed to nothing as I caught sight of a third person on the deck.

Abby Donavan was sitting on the edge of a chaise lounge, holding a wine glass as she said something to Jude. She broke off when I stepped outside.

"Coop. Thanks, man." Logan set down his grill tongs and took the wine from me. "This is good stuff. The girls just finished up some of the white Jude likes, but I'll open this now." He glanced at the women. "Everyone want some Cabernet?"

Jude smiled. "Absolutely." She glanced over at Abby. "Logan, Cooper and I had dinner at a place near Melbourne a few months back, when we all went to check out a house. The bartender recommended this new wine, and we all loved it." She beamed at me. "I can't believe you found it, Coop."

"Yeah, I'm a man of many talents." I tried to keep annoyance out of my voice, but *damn.* I'd been looking forward to a laid-back evening with two of my best friends, the people who were closer to me than almost anyone else in the world. I needed that grounding after the last three weeks of being by turns shook up and uncomfortable over what I'd come to call in my head the Emmy situation.

But now here sat Abby, looking for all the world like she belonged here, too. It wasn't that I didn't like the woman. She'd moved to the Cove . . . I cast my mind back. Hell, it was almost three years ago now. Logan and Jude had hired her to manage the bed and breakfast they'd opened together, and she'd rocked that job. Logan was right that the Cove had needed an upscale, elegant lodging right in town, but we all knew that it was Abby who'd made the Hawthorne House shine. She was a perfectionist, and I'd heard grumblings from some of the workmen who'd come to dread being called to do a job at the B and B. As far as I knew, Abby wasn't a bitch so much as she had high expectations of the people who worked with and for her.

Still, as much as I liked her, she was an outsider. She wasn't one of us, and her being at dinner meant I had to be polite and a little more reserved than normal. I wasn't sure I was up for that tonight.

Jude was continuing to talk, telling the other woman about the house we'd seen in Melbourne the night we'd discovered the wine. That was the way of females, I knew; one thing led to ten more, and they'd be content to chatter about a night and a meal that had happened months back. I barely remembered it myself. I'd stopped for wine tonight on my way here, and I'd just happened to spy that bottle. We didn't need to make it a big deal, and if it were just the three of us, no one would. I held back rolling my eyes as Jude began to describe the décor of the restaurant where we'd eaten. Sometimes I forgot Jude wasn't one of the guys.

"I'm going to help Logan bring out the wine." I knew it was rude, interrupting Jude mid-sentence, but if I waited for a break, I'd be here all freaking night. And it would be ruder to just walk away without an explanation.

Logan had just re-corked the bottle as I wandered into the kitchen. He glanced up at me, and I saw the guilt in his eyes.

Pointing at him, I fixed him with what I hoped was a steely glare. "Not cool, Logan. Not cool at all."

"What?" He spread his hands, like he had no idea what I was talking about.

"Abby?" I hissed her name. I wasn't happy about her being here, but neither did I want to hurt her feelings.

"What about her?" He picked up two glasses and made to move toward the door, but I refused to budge yet.

"Is this some kind of set-up? Like matchmaking? I know your wife, man. She's not going to be happy until all the men in her life are snagged, and as I see it, I'm the last unattached male. This has her fingerprints all over it."

Logan shook his head. "Little paranoid there, Coop? I asked you over here tonight to talk about the Riverside, remember? The hotel? And that's Abby's field. It's her family. Her dad owns and operates one of the most successful boutique hotel chains in the world. So it seemed like a good idea to get her take on the project before we go ahead." He raised his eyebrows. "It's not always about you, Cooper. Maybe you need to get over yourself."

Shit. Had I misread this situation so badly? I was on the verge of groveling, my mouth open to start saying my mea culpas, when I caught Logan watching me out of the corner of his eye, gauging whether or not I was buying his spiel.

"You are full of shit, you know that?" I gave him a little shove. "I almost believed you."

He laughed. "Yeah, well, it wasn't all bull. Jude suggested getting Abby's thoughts about the Riverside, and it sounded like a good idea. It wasn't until just before Ab got here that Jude showed her true hand. Sorry, brother. I wasn't involved in

The Plan

the planning, but I'm not standing in my wife's way when she has a plan."

I sighed. "Logan, I'll tell you. I want to be pissed at you, but there's something about the look on your face every time you refer to Jude as your wife that makes me feel for you, man. You got it bad. I can see that she's got you so twisted up, you'd sell your own mother to make Jude happy. I'll give you a break this one time."

"Yeah, whatever. Just try to behave yourself tonight, and I'll make sure you don't get totally thrown under the bus with Abby." He picked up the wine again, and then paused again. "There's nothing there? With you and Ab, I mean? She's a nice girl, Coop, and she's funny as hell. Smart, pretty and—oh, yeah, sane. That's one of the big things I'd suggest you look for in a woman."

I rolled my eyes. I'd been divorced from Karlee for nearly seven years, and the guys still liked to rib me about that little episode. Even when Matt had bought his Corvette during what we referred to as his midlife crisis, he'd turned to me in the middle of all the joking and said, "At least I can keep mine in the garage. I didn't marry her." *Ouch.*

"You know what? Bite me. I learned my lesson. I'm not looking for a woman—at least, not one to keep around. I like mine in small doses. So yeah, Abby's a peach, and she's fun. But no way am I sniffing around that way. She's a long-term type of girl, and I'm a short-term guy."

Logan lifted one shoulder. "Fine. Grab the other two glasses, please. I need to get back to the grill before our steaks are burnt."

97

I survived dinner. As Logan had said, Abby was sharp, knowledgeable about her job and in possession of a wicked sense of humor. Halfway through the meal, I relaxed and forgot I was there under false pretenses as we debated the pros and cons of the old Riverside.

"But Logan, if you'd seen her from the river, like we did the first time . . . I could just envision it. We'll put in a dock, like they used to back in the day. People can pull up in their boats and stay the night."

I took another sip of wine. "If they have nice boats, why do they want to stay in a hotel? It's like driving an RV and parking it in the lot while you sleep in a hotel."

She waved her hand. "Trust me. No matter how great the boat is, sometimes you want to stay in a real room. Anyway, that's not our main target clientele. The property runs all the way to route 18. If we can get a variance from the town to clear the lot, we can put another entrance right there and bring in more passer-by traffic. That's the one thing that the Hawthorne House doesn't have, being all the way in the middle of town."

Abby nodded. "Not that the Hawthorne needs any more traffic. I have people begging me to bump them up on the waiting list. But I agree about the hotel. Your marketing is going to be aimed at the reservation crowd—the people who plan their trips ahead—along with the impulse people. The ones who're driving down the highway and say, 'Hey, that looks like a cute hotel. Let's check it out.'"

"I think you're jumping the gun when you're talking clients." I stabbed a piece of potato. "This is going to be a huge project, requiring months of work. I thought you were looking for something more like the Hawthorne, just in another town. If you're going to become hoteliers, shouldn't you start small?"

Logan shrugged. "Go big or go home." He lifted Jude's hand, linked with his own, to his lips and kissed her knuckles. "Right, babe?"

Jude smiled. "That's about it." She shifted her gaze to me, some of the softness still lingering in her eyes. "Besides, I need something to keep me busy. Joseph and Lindsay have pretty much taken over the Tide. I'm in there every day, but between the two of them and Sadie and Mack, I'm feeling a little extraneous. I'm not used to having too much time on my hands. When that happens, I get into trouble." She winked at me, and I grinned. No matter how annoyed I might get with Jude from time to time, there was no doubt that I loved her. Like a sister, that is. There'd been a brief time, before she and Logan had declared for one another, when I'd toyed with the idea of Jude and me. On the surface, it'd made sense: neither of us, I'd thought, was looking for big romance. I knew Jude, and it would've been nice to have a date for big events and someone to take to dinner on weekends. She'd let me down gently, telling me that we didn't have the spark, as she called it. While I was willing to forego that kind of nonsense, apparently Jude hadn't been. Sitting here now, watching her with Logan, I remembered her parting words that night.

"Cooper, that spark? Don't give up on it. Not yet. You're go-ing to find someone who can give it to you."

Unbidden, an image of Emmy straddling me, her long red hair a cloud around her beautiful face, rose in my mind. Had that been a spark? Well, it had been something. Something new and different, for sure. I'd been trying to deny it for weeks, trying to convince myself that my night with Emmy hadn't been anything more than my typical hookup.

Spark? I wasn't ready to call it that yet. But it was more than what I felt sitting here chatting with Abby, no matter how pretty and bright she might be. Closer to what I saw be-tween Jude and Logan? Maybe. Still didn't mean I had to act on it. It didn't mean I was going to show up at the Tide this Saturday night for the first time in a month, sit at the bar and try to sweet-talk Emmy Carter into a second go-round.

But it didn't mean I wouldn't, either.

Chapter Five

Emmy

"**I**ZZY, GRAB ME ANOTHER STICK of butter out of the fridge, please." I glanced over my shoulder at my oldest daughter. "I'm elbow deep in dough."

Izzy tossed back her long red braid. "This is the last stick of unsalted." I'd taught all my kids to let me know whenever we used the last of anything, so that I was seldom caught completely without any ingredient.

Still, I hadn't realized we were so close to the end of the butter. "Shit." I muttered the word under my breath. I tried to watch my language around my kids, but I'd long ago decided it was more important to teach them discernment—when was the right time to repeat something Mom had said and when was *not*—than to shelter them completely.

"Want me to go to the market and get some more?" Cameron was sitting at the kitchen table, working on math homework. He looked far too eager for an excuse to close the book. I sympathized, since I'd hated math, too—still did—but first things first.

"Thanks, bud, but this stick'll see me through the last crust, and then I have to make a delivery to the B and B. Finish up that schoolwork, and by the time I'm ready, you can all ride with me. Matt said he had some new boards in if you want to go over there and take a look." Matt Spencer owned The Surf Line, a small shop on the main street of town, across from the Hawthorne House. Eddy had worked for him on and off over the years, and I had a sneaking suspicion that Matt had kept him on more as a favor than because he made any real contribution to the business. After Eddy left town, Matt had delivered a check to me, insisting it was back salary he owed my ex-husband. I was dubious, but Matt wouldn't take no for an answer. At the time, I'd needed every cent I could scrounge up.

In the last few years, Matt had taken my son under his wing. To my relief, Cam didn't seem to have the same hunger for waves that his father did; his passion was surfing sidewalks. Matt had begun stocking skateboards a while ago, and he often invited Cam over to check them out. I was grateful for one more strong male influence on Cameron's life.

My mind was elsewhere, but thanks to muscle memory, my fingers kept the piecrust dough moving. I rolled, smoothed, spread and crimped almost without thinking about it. Once the pie was safely in the oven, I began turning muffins out of tins and sliding Danish pastries from the cookie sheets as I called for reinforcements.

We were a well-oiled machine, my daughters and me.

Dee, who'd just turned six, was a pro at putting together boxes. Once they were assembled, she passed them onto Izzy, who at nine years old was adept at boxing pastries and muffins. She layered them with waxed paper and taped the boxes securely.

By the time the pie was out of the oven and cooling, the week's pastries were ready to go. I stole a peek over Cameron's shoulder and noticed that he was working on the last few math problems. Perfect timing, since the pies needed to cool a little before I moved them to the transporting containers.

I started up the van so that the air conditioner could kick in before the food was loaded. Everyone carried something, securing all the baked goods as we did every week.

"All aboard! This train is leaving for town." The kids giggled as they always did. That was the great thing about having children, I decided: up to a certain point, at least, they were contractually obligated to laugh at Mom's corny jokes. I dreaded to think the day was coming when I'd no longer be funny.

The idea of them getting older reminded me of Lexie Davis, which of course made me think of Cooper. Not that I needed much prodding in that direction these days; for the past month, since our one and only night together, Cooper had been on my mind almost constantly. I didn't go out of my way to either see him or avoid him, but I was thinking it wasn't a coincidence that we hadn't crossed paths in nearly four weeks. He might've insisted we could still be friends, but I had a hunch he didn't want to test that theory.

Town was hopping today. Season was in full swing, and

I bit my lip in concentration as I maneuvered down a side alley, coming up alongside the Hawthorne's service entrance. The small parking lot to the side of the B and B was filled to capacity.

The kids and I had our routine here, too. They helped me carry everything into the kitchen, and then while I had my weekly meeting with Abby—which was usually more of a visit between friends, with a few minutes of business tossed in for good measure—they all dispersed. Cameron would go across the street to hang out with Matt, while the girls usually went right over to the Tide. They loved to play with Lindsay and Joseph's two little ones, who were almost always at the restaurant this time of day. Jude would be there, too, and she'd set my daughters up with a basket of fries while they amused her grandchildren.

"Something smells good!" Abby came into the kitchen as we set down the last boxes. "Did you kids do all this by yourselves?" It was her regular joke with the kids, and they always played along.

"Yeah, you know we're at the stove slaving away while Mom sits on the sofa, eating ice cream and watching trash TV." Cam shook his head, pretending to look sad.

"Brat." I gave his shoulder a little shove. "Go on now, get over to Matt's. I'm not going to be too long here today."

Izzy giggled. "You say that every week, and then you and Miss Abby sit here forever talking. And then you say you didn't think it had gotten so late, and where does the time go?" Dee snickered, too.

I looked at Ab, shaking my head. "Ungrateful wretches."

Sitting down on one of the kitchen stools, I shooed the girls off. "Better get down to Jude's before I tell her no fries for you today."

Dee made a face of mock terror and darted for the door, Izzy following. "Be careful of traffic! Remember it's season." I called the warning mainly for good form; all my kids knew to cross at the corners, and realistically, the volume of cars in town meant they moved at a snail's pace. It was probably safer this time of year than at any other.

Abby poured us each a cup of coffee and slid mine over along with a pitcher of cream. "So. How's your week been? Anything new?"

I poured a splash of milk into my cup, pondering. I hadn't told Abby about my one-night stand with Cooper. I wasn't sure why, except that I just wasn't ready to share that beautiful night with anyone yet, not even with my best friend. Abby and I were close, but we didn't talk about men or our love lives. I assumed that was mostly because neither of us had either of those things in our lives.

I'd met Abby as soon as she'd come to town because Jude had introduced us, strongly suggesting that the new manager of the B and B should hire me to make the pastries and desserts. At the time, I figured Jude's influence had made me a shoe-in for the contract, but once I got to know Abby, I'd realized that she made all her own decisions when it came to business. She could be ruthless, but she was good at what she did. The success of The Hawthorne House was a testament to that.

We'd clicked on another level simply because we were

similar personalities, even though our backgrounds and circumstances were hugely different. Abby was from a large and wealthy hotel family in Philadelphia, and she'd been in the industry for a long time. Why she'd left her family business to come work for Jude and Logan was something she didn't like to talk about, even with me. I had a sense that it had something to do with a man, but I didn't know for sure.

We mostly hung out when I delivered to the B and B, but on occasion, Abby would come over to my house for dinner during the week, if she had coverage at the Hawthorne. My kids loved her, and she was great with them. Neither of us had large chunks of time to socialize, but I considered her the closest friend I had outside Jude, who skirted the line of friendship by also being my boss and surrogate big sister.

"No, nothing new." I answered her question. "Same old, same old. Things are picking up at the Tide. I expect this weekend's going to be a little insane."

Abby nodded. "I bet." She fidgeted, and I narrowed my eyes. It wasn't like her to be distracted.

"So what's new with you?" I leaned onto the counter, resting my chin in my hands.

"Oh, well . . . not much. I had something weird happen last night." Her eyes sparkled a little. "Jude and Logan invited me over to dinner. It's kind of still on the QT, but they're thinking about buying the Riverside Inn and renovating it, and Jude said they wanted my input. I was fine with that, but when I got there, they told me they'd invited Cooper over, too."

My insides jolted, tightening. I swallowed over the huge lump in my throat. "Oh, really?"

"Yeah. But when he got there, I think he was surprised to see me. I don't think they'd told him I was going to be at dinner. Jude didn't say anything, but it felt like a set-up. You know how Jude likes to play matchmaker."

"Uh huh." My head was buzzing. Cooper and Abby. God. How was I going to deal with this? Could I pull off pretending I was happy for her while my heart felt like it was going to pound out of my body?

And Cooper. Mr. No-Relationship-For-Me Davis. What the hell? Was it just me? I was good enough for a hookup, but he wanted the princess for a girlfriend?

I took a deep breath and reined in my runaway brain. Abby was my friend. I loved her, and she was no princess. If she and Cooper clicked, who was I to be anything but happy for them? After all, I'd told Cooper upfront that I didn't want anything serious or long-term. I'd agreed to his parameters as fast as he'd agreed to mine.

We were both idiots.

I managed to speak again. "So how was it? Did you guys . . . you know? Hit it off? Did he ask you out?" *Please say no, please say no, please say no . . .*

Abby hesitated. "No, he didn't ask me out. As for hitting it off, I don't know. I've always liked Cooper, but you know, he's kind of closed off. At first last night, he acted like he'd rather be drowning in the ocean than sitting on that deck with us. With me. He relaxed a little bit as the night went on, but I'm not sure we have any chemistry." She sighed. "Damn shame, too. The man is seriously gorgeous. That face, those eyes—and that body." She fanned herself with her hand. "Maybe we wouldn't be a good match, but I might not say no to a one-night tasting party."

I almost laughed. I wanted to tell her that one night would never be enough with a man like Cooper Davis. But I kept my mouth closed and nodded. "Yeah, Coop's hot. Always has been." I played with the handle of my coffee mug. "I didn't know you were looking for a guy, Ab. Every time I mention a possible man for you, you deflect."

She grimaced. "I'm not. Looking, I mean. I didn't think I was. After—well, I thought I might be done with men for good. Done with relationships. I could be that woman who everyone says is married to her work. Like Elizabeth I."

I giggled, relief beginning to unwind in my chest. "Did you seriously just compare yourself to the Virgin Queen?"

Abby nodded, her lips twitching. "Yup. I totally identify with her. She had all the men groveling at her feet, and she kept them dancing. 'I might marry you . . . or I might not.' That's my role model." She tilted her head. "Plus, she ruled England. Not a bad gig, all things considered."

"You're a nut, you know?" I nudged her with my foot under the counter.

"Yeah, I know." She finished her coffee and pushed away the cup. "In all honesty, I'm not looking for a man in my life. I guess I think if it's meant to be, it's going to have to knock me on my ass, sweep me off my feet and carry me away before I know what's happening. Or I'll find some way to screw it up."

I nodded. "You got hurt pretty bad in Boston, didn't you?" I knew that was where Abby had worked before she moved down here. The flash of surprise on her face confirmed my suspicion.

"It's not that I don't trust you, Emmy. I'm just not ready to talk to anyone about it, even after all this time. Thanks for not pushing me on it."

I patted her arm. "I get it. Besides, I bitch enough about Eddy for the both of us."

Abby's forehead crinkled. "You really don't. I remember when I met you. Jude had told me a little bit of your history, and I expected to meet this harried, bitter woman, trying to hold it all together. Turned out the only part I was on target about was the trying to hold it all together. You rarely say anything about Eddy at all, and God knows you've got cause. I admire you for that, Em. It's one of the reasons your kids are so well-adjusted and independent, too."

"Don't tell them that. I have them fooled into thinking they're still going to need me for a few more years. I need the unpaid labor." I stood up. "Oh, I guess we should talk about what you want for next week. I was thinking blueberry scones and chocolate croissants, and a few mixed berry pies. Does that work?"

"Sounds like a plan." Abby stood up, too. "Thanks, Emmy. See you next week?"

"Sure." I paused in the doorway, looking back at her. "Abby, did Jude come right out and say she was trying to set you up with Cooper? Or was it just a feeling?"

Her cheeks pinked a little. "I asked her as I was leaving. Cooper had taken off while I was helping Jude clean up, so I got the message loud and clear that he wasn't interested. I mentioned something about him, and Jude said she'd thought maybe we'd make a nice couple." Abby shrugged. "It was a sweet idea, but it just didn't work out."

"There's someone out there for you, Abby. You're too wonderful a person to be the next Virgin Queen." I squeezed her arm.

"Hey, right back at you." She cocked her head. "Are *you* looking? You've got a lot to offer, Em."

I opened the door, laughing as I glanced back at her over my shoulder. "Ha. Yeah, three kids, a crazy schedule and what's left of me at the end of the day. I'm hardly the greatest catch out there." Before she could say anything else, I waved. "See you later, lady. Thanks for the coffee."

I made my way around to the front of the big yellow house, turning onto the sidewalk as I headed toward the beach. The Tide rose up to my left; there was a crowd milling just outside the door, which wasn't unusual for this time of year. Tourists wandered in and out of the bar all day. I crossed the street, waving my thanks to the driver of the car who stopped to let me pass.

I didn't bother to go in through the regular door, instead climbing up the wooden steps that led to the deck. Spotting my daughter's red head, I moved in that direction.

"DJ! Try to catch me!" Dee darted just out of the small boy's reach, giggling. The child's dark head bobbed as he tried to catch my daughter. On a chair near them, Izzy was holding little Brenna, Jude's granddaughter.

"Aren't they adorable?" Jude's voice near my ear made me jump. "Brenna loves Izzy. Both the girls are such a help to Lindsay. Maybe we can work out something for them this summer to come over and give her a hand some days."

"They'd love that." I watched the four of them and then glanced at Jude. "I'm surprised to see you here. I thought you were usually off on Thursday afternoons now."

"Most of the time I am. But Lindsay took Brenna for a well-child check today, so I came in to cover for her." She looked over her shoulder toward the inside of the restaurant. "Plus . . . season. I think it's going to be all hands on deck for the next few weeks at least."

"I was just saying the same thing to Abby." I pulled out a chair and sat down, and Jude followed suit. "Speaking of Abby. I heard you were up to old tricks, Miss Jude."

Her face flushed a little, but Jude put on a good show of innocence. "Me? I don't know what you mean."

"Mmmhmmm. Abby ratted you out."

She threw up her hands. "So sue me. I saw two single people in my life, and I thought they might be good together. We had a nice dinner. No harm, no foul."

"True." I looked out over the ocean. The beach was fairly crowded for late afternoon, since it was a pretty day; the sky was blue and the sun still strong. Weather could be a crap shoot this time of year, even here in Florida. Some days were gorgeous and warm, and then it could turn on a dime and be chilly and gray for a week.

"Jude, can I ask you something? How come you never tried to set me up with anyone?"

Her eyes went wide in surprise, and her mouth fell open a little. "Oh, Emmy. I . . . I don't know. I guess it always just seemed like your life is so complete, I figured you weren't interested in another relationship."

"Ah." I nodded. "But Abby looks like she's on the prowl? And Cooper's in the market for a steady girl?"

Jude shifted in her chair, uncomfortable. "I see what you mean. I don't know, Emmy. I honestly never felt like you needed a man in your life. It's not that I don't care about you, sweetie. You know I do."

"I do know. I was just surprised about Abby. And Cooper." Staring out at the sea again, I sighed.

"There wasn't any chemistry."

I turned my head. "What's that?"

"Chemistry. None of it at all between Abby and Coop. I don't know why I didn't see it before. There was like, there was respect, but nothing sizzled." She smirked. "No spark."

I raised one eyebrow. "I think I'm missing something."

Jude laughed. "Oh, it's nothing. Back before Logan and I—well, were Logan and I, Cooper made a move on me. Sort of."

I settled back in my chair. "This I have to hear."

"It was more funny than anything else. I didn't know it at the time, but the posse had decided that Cooper, Matt and Logan would all date me and see if any of us worked out. It sounds silly now, but it was their way of taking care of me after Daniel died." A sad smile curved her lips. "Matt took me out to dinner, and it inspired me to set him up with Sandra. Cooper kissed me one day in his workshop."

"Oh, my God. Cooper *kissed* you? What did you do?" I couldn't imagine Jude and Coop together.

"At first I was shocked. And then I realized that while it was, um, nice, it wasn't setting me on fire."

I wanted to laugh, remembering how I felt the first time Cooper touched my lips with his. Fire? Oh, you betcha. I was basically a crispy timber from that minute on.

" . . . so when he paused, I stopped him from going on. I told him that even though I'd always love him, we didn't have a spark." She touched her lips, as though remembering. "I think even then, although Logan hadn't touched me yet, I already knew I had that spark with him. Cooper said something about us being too old to worry about a spark and I told him that was ridiculous. I wanted to hold out for the spark. And I told him he should hold out for it, too."

Breathing was becoming an issue. All I could remember was the heat between Cooper and me that night. Spark? Oh, yeah. And then some. Spark to spare.

"I always thought Cooper said he was done with relationships."

Jude nodded. "He does say that. And to give him his due, he's had some bad experiences. But I don't think Cooper's washed up yet. There's someone out there for him. Someone who can put up with his bullshit and coax him out of his moods. He can be intense, our Coop. He goes into hiding sometimes, and he needs someone to pull him out of it." She glanced at me. "Someone strong, and tough."

Heat crept up my neck. "I guess that's true." I murmured the words and then pulled out my phone. "Cripes, look at the time. I need to get these kids moving. Izzy still has some homework, and Cam's probably driving Matt bonkers down at the store. I'll just text him to meet us at the van." I stood, pushing in my chair. "Thanks, Jude. Let me know if you and Linds are serious about the girls helping out. They'd be thrilled."

"Will do. See you tomorrow afternoon?" Jude stood up, too, watching me with a small smile playing on her lips.

"Yep, with bells on." I raised my voice to call the girls and hustled them back to our car, all the while thoughts of sparks and kisses and electric blue eyes filled my mind, reminding me that my one-night hookup was far from forgotten.

Chapter Six

Cooper

"OH, MR. DAVIS. OH, MY. It's just . . . oh, my."
The hugely pregnant woman sitting in the
middle of my workshop burst into tears and buried
her face in her hands. She leaned forward, sniffling, and ran one
finger over the smooth wood of the armrest. Behind her, an older
woman dabbed at her own eyes.

"I'm sorry." Blowing her nose, the daughter pushed herself to
stand. "I'm very emotional right now. I'm two weeks overdue, and
the doctors keep telling me the baby will come when he's ready, but
I feel like I've been pregnant forever and everything makes me cry.
Mom kept saying the chair would never be ready by the time we
brought the baby home from the hospital, but now it will be and
it's the first thing that's gone right in months. You have no idea."

I shifted my weight to my other leg. "I get it. I, uh, I have
a daughter. I remember how tough the last weeks were for my
ex-wife."

"Oh, see?" Daughter turned to her mother. "I told you he was a good man." She looked back at me. "Thank you for understanding. Now if we can just load the chair into my—oh!"

There was a loud pop and then a gush, and then there was a puddle under my jigsaw.

"So what did you do?" Matt took a long drink of beer, watching me over the bottle. We were at the Surf Line, which was closed for the night. I came down here sometimes to see him after hours, check in on some of our community projects or just catch up on life. Matt always kept a cooler in the back room, fully stocked with our favorite brews.

I shrugged. "What could I do? I called 9–1–1, got a ton of rags to mop up the mess and then arranged for the chair to be delivered to her house. It'll be there when she gets home with the baby." I tipped back my beer and then added, "It was a boy. Ten pounds, eight ounces, twenty-two inches long."

"Holy shit. That poor woman." Matt shuddered. "Well, at least the chair's done and out of your hair."

"Yeah, and I already arranged for a hazmat cleaning service to come over to take care of my workshop floor."

Matt laughed. "Dude, you're a father. I'd think you'd be used to that kind of shit."

I shook my head. "Lex is so old now, I've blocked all that other stuff out of my head. It no longer exists for me."

"Yeah, well . . ." He ducked his head. "I guess I need to start thinking about it. Sandra's pregnant."

It took me a minute to process what he was saying, and then a whoosh of gladness overwhelmed me. "Oh my God, man. Congratulations. Holy crap. You're going to be a dad."

"I know." He grinned. "We've known for a little bit, but Sandra asked me not to say anything until she got through the first trimester. Now it looks like it's going to stick, so I'm allowed to spread the news."

"I don't know if I'm more shocked that you're going to be a father or that you kept a secret that long, blabber Matt." I poked him in the ribs, remembering his old nickname.

"There's actually more. Sandra and I got married as soon as we found out."

"What the fuck!" I pulled out a display cube and dropped onto it. "So you're married and you're pregnant? And you're just now telling me. Where did you get married?"

He sat, too. "We drove to the Keys and got married at a little church down there. It was just the two of us, no one else. But I've known for a long time that I wanted her to be my wife, and whether or not the pregnancy stuck, I knew I wanted to. Stick, I mean."

"Am I the first one you're telling?"

Matt nodded. "Yeah. I'll let everyone else know over the next few days. We're going to have some kind of party or something to celebrate, but I wanted you to hear it from me." He stood up. "Now if you don't mind, I hate to cut this short, but I need to get home. Sandra's still getting over all the puking, and evenings are rough on her."

"Sure thing." I clapped him on the shoulder. "I'm happy for you, Matt. Really. Nobody deserves it more than you."

We parted outside the store, and I stood next to my Jeep for a minute, watching the taillights of Matt's car disappear down the road. Turning my head, I glanced toward the beach, where the lights from the Tide glowed bright, tempting me. I knew Emmy was in there, working the bar. I knew if I went inside, sat down, nothing would stop me from having her again tonight. As sure as I was standing here in the dark, I'd end up going home with her.

I pushed off the car and made my way up the sidewalk, winding around all the people milling there. Since it was Saturday night, the music tonight would be live, and the crowds would be huge. I could hear the DJ who opened up on Saturdays playing something loud and country.

The bar was filled, but I managed to wedge myself between two groups. One of the waitresses, Seline, waved at me and came down to take my order. "Hey, Cooper. What're you doing here?"

I frowned. Had Emmy told her about us? Why shouldn't I be here? Seline must have seen the confusion on my face because she hastened to add, "I mean, we don't see many locals during season."

"Oh." I nodded. "Well, I was down having a beer with Matt, and I thought I'd just come and see who's playing tonight. I don't usually get to see the live bands."

"Well, you're in for a treat tonight. This group's just about explode. They're a country band out of Alabama, and Mason—Meghan's friend from up in Georgia? He hooked us up with them. Emmy's really excited about it."

"That's great." Country music. It wasn't my favorite, and I tried not to wince. "So speaking of Em, is she around?"

Seline glanced over her shoulder. "Yeah, she's here somewhere. Probably talking to the band or their manager." She smiled at me. "What can I get you to drink?"

"Just a beer, please. Whatever you've got handy on tap."

"Coming right up." She turned to fill my order, and I let my eyes wander over everyone else at the bar, searching as subtly as I could for a red head. There were blondes galore, girls from their teens on up through middle age. More than a few brunettes. A few of the girls tried to catch my eye, but I didn't let my gaze linger anywhere. I wasn't interested in anyone but the woman I'd come here to see.

Seline delivered my beer and waved as she skittered to the other side of the bar to take more orders. I watched her absently; she picked up an empty wine glass, and just then a group of people moved away, giving me a better view. I spotted the red hair I'd been searching for. And then my heart seized.

Because Emmy was there, seated far too intimately next to a tall man with blond hair, artfully mussed in that way that made it look like he didn't care—although of course he did. This guy was staring into her eyes, one hand on her shoulder. Those fingers were moving over Emmy's skin, caressing the part exposed by her clinging tank top. His other hand was at her waist, just resting there, curled over her hip. She had one of her small white hands on his tanned arm, and she was smiling as she spoke to him.

My blood boiled. I always thought that was an expression, but now I knew what it meant. I wanted to grab this guy by the back of his neck and fling him away from Emmy, hit him right in his perfect nose.

Son of a bitch.

Before I knew what I was doing, I was pushing through the crowd, my eyes never leaving Emmy. Right as I drew up

119

to them, the guy with his hands all over my girl saw me. His smile faded a little when he recognized the look in my eyes, I guessed, because he pulled back a little from Emmy and jerked his head in my direction.

Emmy glanced around at me, and the flare I saw in her eyes burned down to make my cock go hard. She straightened up but didn't move away from dickface.

"Hey, Cooper." The cool tone in her voice belied the fire I'd just seen on her face. "What're you doing here?"

"Who's this?" I hooked my thumb in the direction of the handsy blond.

He leaned around Emmy and extended one of those hands, smiling at me like we were about to become best friends. "Hi, I'm Alex Nelson. I'm a friend of Meghan's from Georgia."

"Yeah." I didn't want to shake his hand, but he didn't move back, and finally I realized I didn't have a choice. Up close, I could see this guy was closer to Meggie's age than to Emmy's. He couldn't be more than twenty-five or twenty-six. Still, Emmy didn't look like she was much older.

She shot me a look that promised imminent murder. "Alex is down here on business, and since Mason set up tonight's band, he came in as a favor to make sure everything runs smoothly." She turned back to Alex and smiled, this time with real warmth. "Alex, this is Cooper Davis. Don't let his rudeness throw you. He's a friend of Jude and Logan's."

I noticed she didn't include herself in that sentiment. Fine, I didn't want to be her friend anymore anyway.

"Oh, *Cooper?*" The dude's eyes got real big. "You're the

one who made Meghan and Sam that beautiful chest as an engagement gift, aren't you? Oh my God, it's a work of art. I told my boyfriend about it, and he said he'd heard of you." He hunched down a little and lowered his voice. "He's an art dealer, so he knows more about that stuff than me. I'm basically a philistine, but I know what I like."

As his words filtered into my brain, I felt tension drain from my neck and shoulders. *Boyfriend.* Suddenly the way Alex had his arm draped over Emmy's shoulder didn't make me want to break it off and beat him.

"Emmy?" A guy wearing jeans and a long flannel shirt came over to us. "We're ready to go on, whenever you're ready to announce us."

"Perfect. I'll do that now." She patted Alex's cheek as she stepped away, pausing just long enough to look over her shoulder at me. "Cooper, are you staying for the show?"

Country music. Seriously? I took in Emmy's bright eyes, red hair curling around her face, and the way the thin cotton of her tank hugged those luscious breasts. Yeah, I could tolerate some twang and whining for that. "Yeah, I'm staying." I lifted one eyebrow and smirked. "Actually, I wouldn't miss it."

Her expression didn't change, but she gave me a brief nod and pivoted to walk away. I leaned against the bar, watching her go.

"So. How long've you been tapping that?" Alex grinned at me.

"What? No, I . . . wait, how'd you know?" Here I thought I'd been so careful about what I said and how I acted around her.

He punched my shoulder. "It's a sixth sense thing. I saw her face the minute she spotted you—her color went up two levels, her heart rate skyrocketed and her temperature, too, I'm pretty sure. And you looked at me like you wanted to do bodily harm. Plus, the sparks between you two—whoo, baby. I've seen that before."

I rubbed my jaw. "We're not exactly—well, we had a one-night thing."

"When was that?"

"A month ago."

Alex laughed. "Yeah, well, I don't think you got her out of your system, buddy. And who can blame you? Look at her. Let me tell you, if I didn't dig the dudes, I'd be giving you serious competition."

I rolled my eyes. "You're a little young for her, aren't you?"

"Age is just a number, my man."

Anything else Alex was going to say was lost in a drumroll. Emmy stood in the middle of the small stage on one side of the restaurant, and as all attention turned her way, the room was filled with whistles and catcalls. She shook her head, smiling.

"Okay, y'all. Enough of your nonsense! I want your attention right here—"

"You got my attention, baby!" A man in a baseball cap cupped his hands and yelled. "And anything else of mine you want, too."

I balled my fists, but Emmy handled it, shaking her head. "Simmer down there. Thanks for being here tonight at the Riptide. On behalf of Jude and the whole staff, I'd like to welcome tonight's band. They're from a sweet little town in

Alabama, and their first single is going to debut tomorrow in the top ten of the country chart. We were lucky enough to snag them now—in a few months, y'all are going to have to pay big bucks to enjoy their music. Ladies and gentlemen, and you there in the hat—" There was a wave of laughter. "Put your hands together and give a big Crystal Cove welcome to Tumbleweed!"

The bar shook with the vibration of the yelling and screams. Alex covered his ears, laughing, and I found myself hoping I wasn't doing permanent damage to my eardrums. The band took the stage and immediately launched into their first number.

I hung in there for the first three songs, and I had to admit, they weren't bad, for a country band. The lyrics were more poetry than I expected, and the vocals didn't have the twang I was used to hearing.

They slowed things down for the fourth song, and I spied Emmy leaning against the wall on the other side of the bar. Strands of hair were blowing around her flushed face, and the glow of the lowlights shone on her eyes. Intense need pulsed between my legs. I needed to get to her, and now.

The rest of the room only had eyes for the band, so it wasn't too hard to push past them. She didn't see me right away, not until I'd nearly reached her. Her eyes fastened on mine, and she didn't look away.

I laid one hand on her shoulder and trailed it down her arm. She shivered, despite the heat of the room and the press of bodies around us. I slid my hand into hers and leaned to whisper in her ear.

"Step outside with me for a minute."

She hesitated, looking back up at the stage. I could see her weighing her responsibilities against her desires. Finally she looked back at me and nodded. "Five minutes, tops. They'll be getting to the end of this set by then."

I didn't wait. I tugged her hand and led her to the back door that opened onto the deck.

The cooler air hit me like a wave of refreshing water. I didn't stop until we'd reached the far end of the wooden platform, and then I turned Emmy around and pressed her against the railing.

The darkness around us was black velvet, and a million stars glittered in the clear sky. I couldn't see the ocean, but I could hear waves crashing onto the sand. None of it mattered, though. Nothing mattered but Emmy and getting my mouth on her. Touching her.

Gripping her tight little ass, I ground my body against hers until she moaned and dropped her head back. I took advantage of that position and used my lips to map a trail up her exposed neck until I reached her lips. Touching my tongue to one corner of her mouth and then to the other, I paused, lifting my head to drink in the view of Emmy, in my arms, totally surrendered to me.

I took her mouth then, desperately, like I'd been without my one sustaining force for far too long. Emmy made a small noise in the back of her throat, and I swallowed it, sucking her lower lip between my teeth and nibbling it. I skimmed my hands to her hips, up her sides, spanning her rib cage and letting my thumbs tease the bottom of her breasts through the tank top.

Dragging my lips away from her mouth, I whispered into her ear. "Emmy. Let me come home with you tonight."

She tensed, freezing for a beat, and then I felt her swallow, hard. Her chest rose and fell in rapid breaths, and I thought my heart had stopped beating while I waited.

"Yes." She breathed her answer and lifted her hands to pull my head back down to hers. Her kiss was aggressive and bold, although it ended too soon for me.

"I have to go back in. They'll need me when the set ends, and I have all my regular stuff to do." She rested her hands on my chest, her fingers tracing the ridges of my muscles, making them jump. "Do you want me to call you when I'm done? I know you don't like this kind of music."

"How do you know that?" I leaned my forehead against her, needed to be closer.

She lifted one shoulder. "You said it once. I told you, I have a gift for remembering things people say. Their preferences. It's a bartender thing."

"Hmmm." I kissed her again, fast and hard. "No, I'm not leaving until you do. I'll stay and help you close up."

She looked up into my eyes, and something bright glowed there. "Thank you. I—I need to go back in. Find me after."

And then she was gone. I heard the brief roar as she opened the door, letting the noise and light spill onto the deck. I took a few minutes to calm down my aching body before I followed her inside, one thought pulsing in my mind.

Tonight. Tonight I'd be with her again.

125

"I thought they'd never leave." I swiveled on my bar stool, watching Emmy as she stretched her back. The material over her boobs pulled tight, and coincidentally, so did the fabric covering my crotch.

"Saturdays are always later. And in season? They're all on vacation. No one wants to go home. Or back to their hotels, whatever. They'd stay all night if I kept pulling beers and playing music."

"The band went over well." I'd listened to the second set, surprised to find how much I enjoyed it.

"Oh, yeah." She smiled. "This was a huge deal for us, to have these guys play the Tide. Tomorrow, when their song plays on thousands of country music stations as part of the top ten, they'll be nearly impossible to book, and definitely not for a tiny place like us. I owe Mason big." Emmy began punching numbers on the register, running the report.

"Remind me who Mason is again?" I'd heard his name before, and I had a vague idea that he was someone Jude's daughter Meghan had met up in Georgia, where she lived now with her fiancé.

Emmy leaned her hip against the bar, her eyes on the register display. "Holy shit, we made bank tonight. Jude's going to be very happy." She glanced back at me, distracted. "Oh, Mason? He owns a big bar and dance club up in Burton. He was a friend of Sam's, I guess, growing up, and now he and his wife are pretty close with Meggie, too."

"Ah." I nodded. "Okay, want me to check the kitchen?"

"Sure."

We both focused on our chores, the silence between us

companionable rather than tense. I liked this feeling. I could get used to it, I mused. Maybe I could handle something a little more defined with Emmy. Something more than a hookup, and something less than a commitment. Meeting on Saturday nights, going home with her after I helped her close up—I could work with that.

It was little déjà vu, leaving the Tide with Emmy, following her back to her house. But when we both stood in her living room, a hint of awkward crept in. Emmy bit her lip, her eyes on the floor.

"Do you want to go back to my bedroom?"

"How about a glass of wine?"

We both spoke at the same time, and then laughed. Emmy turned toward the kitchen. "Wine sounds like an excellent idea. Come on."

"Hey, I liked your suggestion, too." I sat down, straddling the chair.

"I didn't mean to sound like that's all I wanted." She poured us each a glass of her favorite red and corked the bottle. "I just thought that's how you wanted it. Sex, and nothing else."

I blew out a sigh. "Emmy, I'm not a nice person. I know I've said that before, but it's true. I was upfront with you last time, and you were with me, too. But maybe there's more to this—to us—than just a hookup. That night—it was incredible. I've been avoiding you since then because I didn't know how to deal with how much it meant to me." I took a sip of the wine she'd set down in front of me. "Tonight I couldn't stay away anymore, but that doesn't mean I've changed what

I am. Who I am. I still don't do relationships. But what if we made this more of a regular thing? You know, like friends with benefits. No one has to know. But maybe it'd be good for both of us."

Emmy regarded me, her gaze steady but inscrutable. "Friends with benefits." Her voice held a vague tinge of irony, but she nodded slowly. "What would that look like? We call each other whenever we're in the mood for sex?"

"In theory, yes. But given your schedule, it might work better if we just planned to meet every Saturday, like tonight."

Emmy sat down, her face still expressionless. "Okay. Every Saturday? What if you have Lexie overnight?"

I shrugged. "Then we adjust. I'm not saying I have this all worked out. It was just an idea."

"I see." Em leaned forward in her chair, reaching back to rub her shoulder. "God, my back hurts tonight. It must be tension, worrying about the band getting there and set up."

"You need a massage." I stood up and moved behind her, brushing her hands out of the way as mine took their place. "Drop your head onto your chest. Yeah, just like that." I lifted her hair off her back, draping it to hang forward over her shoulder, and rubbed the bare skin between the top of her shirt and her neck. She hummed a little in pleasure as I dug my thumbs into the knotted muscles.

"Right there. Yeah, that's the spot. Oh, God—yes. Right—yes."

She sounded way too erotic right now, and my cock was definitely paying attention. I slipped my fingers under the material of her shirt, running them down her spine until she

shivered and then bringing them back up to continue working her tight shoulders.

When she seemed to be totally relaxed, I leaned down,
sliding my hands into the front of her shirt to palm her tits.
The sound she made threatened to undo me. I tugged the
cups of her bra out of the way, desperate to find her nipples.
When my fingers began to roll the stiff peaks, she arched, her
hips moving up and away from the chair.

I bent and lifted her into my arms, finding her mouth
as I carried her to the bedroom, just as I had last time. I'd
never carried a woman before Emmy, I realized, but there was
something so perfect about having her body tucked against
my chest, her head on my shoulder and her mouth under
mine.

In the bedroom, I laid her across the mattress and
stripped off my clothes. Emmy's eyes opened halfway, watching me with a smile.

"I think this time, I'm the one who has on too many
clothes. But I'm too relaxed to take them off." She rolled her
head to look at me as my knee made the bed dip. "Any ideas
of how to make this work?"

"I think I might have one or two." I pulled at the hem of
her tank top and stripped it from her, making short work of
her bra after that. She lay in only her shorts, making it easy
for me to unbutton them and slip them down her legs and
onto the floor.

"Now what?" Her whisper tantalized me.

"Now, I make you feel good." I dipped my head to capture one rosy-tipped breast. Emmy gasped and gripped the

back of my head with her hand, pressing me closer. When I moved to the other side, I replaced my mouth with my fingers, teasing and tweaking.

"Tell me, baby. Tell me what you want." I licked the lobe of her ear as I murmured. "Tell me, and I'll make it happen."

"I want you . . . between my legs. Lick me, Cooper. Make me come like that."

My mouth curled into a smile. "I can do that." I slithered down her body, pausing at crucial spots to suck, lick and bite gently. When I lay between her legs, I turned my head to run my mouth over the soft skin of her inner thighs, blowing on her between kisses, moving closer to the wet heat of her core until she was trembling. I parted her with one finger and brought my lips to her clit.

"Yes. There. Oh, God, Cooper. Harder, please. Harder."

I sucked at her, bringing the small bundle of nerves into my mouth and using my tongue to press hard. Emmy groaned, her hand against the back of my neck. As if I were going anywhere.

I could tell she was getting close. Without moving my mouth, I plunged two fingers into her, pumping them in and out, hitting the spot that made her cry out my name.

"That's it, baby. Come for me now. Come against my mouth, Em. Ride my hand and come into my mouth."

Whether it was the feel of my voice against her or the words I spoke, something seemed to push her over the edge. She arched, lifting her hips as her channel clenched hard on my fingers. I stayed with her, moving slower and stroking to bring her down.

I expected her to be sated and limp as I kissed her stomach, but instead Emmy gripped my shoulders.

"Roll over." There was something in her voice, an authority that I had zero desire to disobey. I flipped to my back, watching as she leaned over me, her hair hanging in a curtain around us.

"It's my turn to be in charge, Cooper." Her hands roamed over my chest, down my arms and teased the skin on my stomach, just barely avoiding my throbbing cock. "Do as I say and no one gets hurt."

I grinned. "Em, baby, you had me at 'in charge.'"

She laughed, soft and sweet. "I want to make you feel so damn good." Her hand gripped the base of my erection, fisting up and down a few times before she bent and took me into her mouth.

There was nothing shy or halting about this. Emmy's mouth consumed me, sucking so hard I thought my eyes would cross. She trailed her tongue down the sensitive underside and then took me deep, swallowing so that the head of my dick hit the back of her throat.

Just when I thought I couldn't take another second without coming hard into her beguiling mouth, Emmy sat up, slung one leg over my hips and positioned herself above me. She held my cock near her entrance, rubbing the head over her own swollen flesh.

"Cooper, are you clean?" She asked the question in a breathless voice.

"What?" I was so intent on her hands and mouth on my body that I had trouble figuring out what she meant. "Oh.

Yeah. I haven't been with any woman without a condom since my first divorce. Tested, too. Healthy. Ohhhh, God, Emmy . . ."

I spoke the last words in a long groan as she sank down onto my cock, taking me deep and sure into her body. Leaning her hands on my chest, she whispered to me. "I had my tubes tied after Dee was born. We're safe. I wanted to feel you in me, with nothing between us." She rocked, lifting her hips and then dropped back onto me. "It's incredible."

She was right. It was more than incredible; it felt like nothing I'd ever experienced, my dick bare inside Emmy's tight little pussy. I wanted to stay like this for the rest of my life. I wanted to feel her sliding herself up and down on me, finding her rhythm, her beautiful tits in my face, for fucking ever.

I lifted my head to suck one of her nipples into my mouth, and Emmy hissed. I could tell she was trying to find her own pleasure, which was fine with me, as long as she kept up the search as she was now, moving different ways, circling her hips, grinding against me.

"Touch yourself, baby." I knew she needed that permission to find her own release. "Touch your clit while you ride me. Oh, God, Emmy. You keep doing that—it's making me fucking nuts. I fucking love that, baby. Oh—God, yes."

She sat up a little, slipping two fingers between her legs. I watched her press against her clit, felt her knees tightened at my waist as she surrendered to the pace that had found her. Digging my fingers into her clenched thighs, I let the orgasm sweep over my body, destroying me. Emmy dropped down against me as I came hard into her. She ground herself on me, making the most delectable little noises as she climaxed with a shudder and a gasp.

She fell onto my chest, her ribs heaving as she panted. I wrapped my arms around her, holding her as tight as I could, and tried to remember why doing this—with her—all the time wasn't the very best idea I'd ever had.

Chapter Seven

Emmy

THE BEACH WAS PERFECTION TODAY, I decided. The air was soft with spring, the sun was warm, and the breeze was constant enough to make sure we weren't too warm. As I sat on our blanket, staring into the waves, I congratulated myself on having the idea to spend the afternoon here.

Vacations were not something that ever fit into either our schedule or our budget. That was why I was particularly grateful that we lived at the beach, where an afternoon mini-vacay was only moments away from home and cost us nothing. My kids loved the sand and the water, and all three were good swimmers already, thanks to Eddy. That was one gift my ex had given them, and I appreciated it.

I hadn't planned today's beach trip until I'd gotten into the car to pick up the kids from my parents' house that morning. When I made the suggestion on our way home, it was met with cheers and excitement. Everyone pitched in to make it happen: the girls made us a picnic lunch and Cam packed the beach bag with towels, sand toys and sunscreen. We all changed into bathing suits and were in the sand before the hour was out.

They were all playing in the surf now, their laughter ringing across the light wind. I loved to watch them jump and squeal with total abandon since it reassured me that they really were happy children, that I wasn't giving them too much responsibility and too many chores. Cam splashed Izzy, and Dee dropped onto her bottom, landing in the wet sand. Yeah, there was no doubt they'd needed this.

I'd needed it, too.

Cooper hadn't stayed over last night. I'd dozed a few minutes after my earth-shattering orgasm, and when I'd woken up, he was moving me carefully off his body.

"I'm afraid I'm going to fall asleep." He'd softened his words with a kiss to my forehead. "You have to get your kids in the morning, and I'm supposed to meet Lex and Jolie for breakfast, so I can take Lex back to my house for the day. I better go." He'd dropped to his knees next to my bed, his face level with mine. "I wish I didn't have to."

I believed he meant it. But even though it made total sense—he was right, I did have to get the kids this morning—I wanted him to stay. Having him leave in the middle of the night made me feel like what we were doing was shameful and cheap. Like I wasn't worth staying the night.

So when he bent over me, brushing hair from my face, and whispered that he'd see me next weekend, I shook my head.

"I can't do this, Cooper. God, I wish I could. I wish I was built that way. But I can't just sleep with you on Saturday nights and pretend it doesn't mean anything the other six days of the week."

He'd straightened, slowly, and nodded. I wanted him to argue with me, to tell me I was wrong. To say it meant more. But he didn't. Without saying anything else, he touched my cheek and left me.

The wind picked up a little, tossing sand against my face. Squinting my eyes, I turned my head, looking down the shoreline. The afternoon was waning, and since it was a Sunday, most families and tourists had either left or were packing up. But one couple lingered near the water, holding hands as they walked. As I watched, the man halted, tugging the woman against his chest. He slid both of his hands up to her face, cupping her cheeks as he lowered his mouth to hers. Her arms lifted, her hands linking behind his neck.

Watching them, I felt as though I were intruding on something intimate and precious. And it hit me, suddenly and with a force that left me breathless, that I wanted that. I wanted what these two strangers on the beach shared. I had no idea how long they'd been together, whether they'd met yesterday or twenty-five years ago, but I could sense their connection even from here. I felt that with Cooper. I was comfortable with him on every level, and I wanted to be near him, all the time.

And I didn't want to hide our connection. I wanted to walk on the beach with him, kiss him until we were both crazy with need, without worrying about what anyone else might think. I wanted to sit here in the sand, with my back against his broad chest, his arms loose around me as we watched my kids play in the breaking waves. I wanted to be able to talk with Lexie and know she was okay with her father and me together. I wanted to go with him to the posse get-togethers, have him pull me to him when I walked past, kiss me hot while he grabbed my ass, just as I'd seen Logan do to Jude.

But I had to face facts, and those facts told me that Cooper wasn't looking for any of that. He liked what happened between us in bed. I was fairly certain he liked me out of bed, too. And there wasn't any doubt he didn't like other guys paying attention to me, if his hostile reaction to Alex last night had been any indication. But he didn't care enough to make sure the world knew I belonged to him, and he didn't care enough to disrupt his carefully put-together life to include me.

"Mommy, will you help me build a sand castle?" Dee had tired of running in the water. She plopped onto the blanket with me, digging in the bag for a shovel.

"Of course, baby." I put on a smile and twisted to face her. We smoothed out a square of sand and then dug a deep hole to find wet sand. "If we want it to stand, we need to build a strong foundation before we add height. Let's use this."

As we worked, resolution took hold, and I knew what I had to do. I wasn't going to get what I wanted, what I'd seen in that other couple, with Cooper. Not the way things were now, when he was happy just to count on me for regular sex. If I wanted commitment and security, happiness on a level that I'd seen in others, I had to find it myself. I had a good idea about where to start.

The Tide was relatively quiet on Monday afternoon when I pushed open the door. There were a few families sitting at tables, and a couple of Jude's regular fishermen at the bar nursing their daily beers, but it was nothing like the hustle we'd seen this weekend or how busy it would get later in the week.

Jude stood behind the bar, leaning against a column with her arms crossed as she chatted with the fishermen. When she spotted me, her smile grew to spread across her face. "Well, if it isn't the entertainment maven of Crystal Cove! Girl, you kicked ass Saturday night."

I grinned. "Liked those receipts, did you?"

"I did." She glanced at the men at the bar. "Can you guys fend for yourselves for a few minutes? Sadie's around here somewhere if you need something." Pushing off the wall, she inclined her head toward the door that led to the deck. "Come sit down for a minute."

We sat looking out over the beach. Jude slid the sunglasses from the top of her head down over her eyes. "I'm glad you came in today. I was going to call you and see if we could talk this week."

A seed of panic settled in my chest. "Really? Why? Everything okay?"

Jude smiled and reached across the table to squeeze my arm. "Emmy, relax. Everything's fine. I just wanted to tell you how excited we were about this weekend. I think it was the biggest weekend the Tide's ever had, in all its history." She paused and sat forward to pull something out of her back pocket. "Logan and I've been talking about this for a long time, and I should've done it earlier. Em, we want you to start taking a percentage of the weekend profits. What you've done for weekends here has been nothing short of miraculous. You should reap some of the benefits." She laid a long white envelope on the table and slid it toward me. "This check is from the past weekend. With our thanks."

I didn't move for a minute, and Jude gave me a little kick under the table. "Take it. It's not going to bite."

Picking up the envelope, I slit the top with my finger and glanced in at the amount box on the check. My heart pounded, and my head swam. For a minute, I really thought I might pass out. "Holy shit, Jude. Are you fucking crazy?"

Jude laughed, throwing her head back. "No, I'm not. What's crazy is that I didn't do this a year ago. I'm sorry, Em. It was never that I didn't think you deserved a percentage deal, or that you weren't worth it. But you know what it's like. When you're on your own, running a business that has to support your family, you tend to get a little . . . possessive. I was looking at the fact that the Tide now has to support not only me, but Joseph and Lindsay, too." She shook her head, smiling ruefully. "Logan had to smack me upside the head. He reminded me that I'm not on my own anymore, and that we don't need the Tide to support us. Between his income and what we make in Holt/Hawthorne, we're very blessed. So maybe it's time for the Tide's profits to benefit you—and Joseph's family, too, of course."

"Jude, I just don't know what to say." My hands were shaking. "This is . . . it's huge. It's life-changing for me. You have no idea."

"Oh, I think I do." She regarded me steadily. "I'll never forget the day you came in here, Emmy, bringing the pies I'd ordered and telling me I needed to hire you as night manager. I already admired the hell out of you, but that day I knew you had balls to spare. Not many women could pull off what you've done. I'm proud of you, Em."

Tears sprang to my eyes, and I blinked them back furiously. "I couldn't have done any of this without you. And Daniel, and Logan, and . . . well, my mom and dad, of course. But you trusted me, Jude. You took a chance on me, first with the pies and then with the Tide. I owe you everything."

"No, you don't." She shook her head. "Yes, we gave you a shot. But you pointed out what you could do for us, and when we let you try, it was you who worked your ass off to make it succeed. You gave it everything you have. Own it, Em. Be proud."

I nodded and turned my head to look out over the ocean. Jude must've sensed I needed a minute, because she was quiet for a little while. When she spoke, her voice was lighter, almost teasing.

"I kind of hijacked you the second you came in. Was there something you wanted to talk about? God, please don't say you came to give me your notice."

Laughing, I shook my head. "No, not hardly. Actually, what I wanted to talk to you about doesn't have anything to do with work." I played with the corner of the envelope that still lay on the table. "Jude, would you set me up with some-one? Like, on a date? A blind date?"

The expression of utter shock on her face would've been funny if I hadn't been so nervous. Jude's eyes went wide, and when she opened her mouth, nothing came out for a moment. I hurried to explain.

"I was thinking about what you said the other day, that you never felt like I needed another man in my life. And maybe I don't need a man, but I think I want one. I don't want to get to the point where the kids are grown and gone, and I'm suddenly alone."

Jude nodded. "Of course. Did you—um, did you have anyone special in mind?"

"No." I couldn't meet her eyes. "I was hoping you and Logan might know someone."

"Okay. What exactly are you looking for in a man?" Jude watched me carefully, as though she already knew the answer and was just checking to make sure I did, too.

"Someone who's interested in a relationship." That was a big one, since it was the one thing Cooper couldn't offer me. "Someone who won't mind my kids. Or even might like them. Oh, and please, no surfers."

"Ha! No worries there." Jude laughed. "What about physical traits? Do you have a type?"

I never thought I did, but immediately a man with short dark hair and intense blue eyes came to mind. With a frown, I pushed him aside. "Not really. I mean, if George Clooney's available, I wouldn't say no. Or eTatum. Oooh, or Jesse Williams."

"Good to see your standards and expectations aren't too high. Okay, let me think about it a little while." She hesitated. "Emmy, you're sure about this? There's . . . no one else who you might be interested in? Who you already know?"

I felt the blush rising on my face. *God, what had she heard?* It didn't matter, because the temporary insanity that was Cooper and me was over. I needed to take care of me, and a big part of that was finding a man I could trust, whose goals were like mine. Someone to hold me at night and be my date and sit with me on the beach at sunset.

"No one who wants the same things I do." I set my jaw. "Nobody who's interested in the long-term."

Jude leaned across the table again, this time gripping my hand. "I understand, Em. Give me a day or two, and I'll find just the man."

I forced a smile. "Thanks, Jude. I knew I could count on you."

~⊙~

Jude was as good as her word. On Wednesday morning, I was just finishing up a pie order when my phone rang.

"Get ready, girl. I got you a man."

I fit the phone between my ear and shoulder. "Wow, you work fast."

She laughed. "I do. Are you free Thursday night?"

"Thursday . . ." I cast my mind forward, trying to think. "I'll have to see if my mom can watch the kids, but other than that, yeah."

"If she can't, I'll come over and sit with them. Or they can come hang out with me. They love Logan's pool table."

"Oh, thanks. Now tell me about this guy."

"He's perfect, Em. He's an attorney, and his office is in Logan's building. They've worked together before—Logan's given expert testimony for some of Travis's cases, and Travis has looked over some of our deals for Holt/Hawthorne."

"Travis?" I tried out the name. *Travis.* Could that be a name I'd call out in passion, as he lay with his head between my legs? I shook my head, frowning in annoyance with myself. Travis sounded like someone I could walk with on the beach. Someone who could hold his own with my kids.

"I set everything up," Jude was saying. "He's going to meet you at six out at Stefano's." The Italian restaurant was in Elson, the next town inland. "I figured that way you don't have to worry about running into anyone you know from the Cove."

"Oh, that's a good idea." The last thing I wanted was to see Cooper while I was out on a blind date. "How will I know him?"

"He's going to meet you in the front. He's got dark hair, and he's fairly tall. I told him what you look like, so I don't think you'll have any problem finding each other."

"Okay." I blew out a long breath. "So I guess I'm really doing this."

"At least you only have two days to work up a good nervous about the date. I figured it was better to act fast than to give you time to second guess yourself."

Jude was right, but I did manage to worry myself into a

wreck over the next twenty-four hours anyway. My parents were more than willing to come over and sit with the kids when I told them what I was doing, and they made a fuss over me as I came out of my room.

"Oh, look how pretty you are!" My mom clasped her hands together, smiling. "I can't remember the last time I saw you in a dress, sweetie. You're breathtaking."

"Do we have this guy's name? His phone number? The license plate of his car?" My father was suspicious. He was out of practice, since I hadn't gone on a date with a new guy since I was fifteen. And look how that had turned out.

"Daddy, it's fine. Jude and Logan know him. I'm sure they have all his pertinent information and maybe even an extra key to the dungeon where he locks up women for his . . . experiments." I raised my eyebrow, but my father just shook his head.

"You can yuck it up, Em, but I watch the news. I watch *Dateline*. I know what goes on. Does your cell phone have a tracker on it? Does your mother know how to use it?"

I picked up my keys and purse. "Thanks, Mom, for doing this. Daddy, I'll check in by text every fifteen minutes. If I miss one, you can send out the cops." I kissed the girls and ruffled Cam's hair. "Keep it down to a low roar, you guys. Love you."

The drive over the bridge out to Elson only took about fifteen minutes. I was a little early, and I took a deep breath as I walked toward the porch. A man leaned against one of the posts, hands in the pockets of his khakis. His brown hair was a little long, skimming his collar, and when he glanced up, I saw his eyes were dark.

Good. No blue eyes. I couldn't handle a date where I spent the whole time comparing the guy to—someone else. If this was Travis, I'd be okay. His height was average, and he wasn't bad looking. He seemed . . . I debated the right words. Comfortable. Easy. And wasn't that just what I wanted?

"Emmy?" He spoke my name as I climbed the steps.

"Yeah, hi. You must be Travis?" I offered my hand, which he took in both of his. I should've found that gesture charming, but instead it felt like a little too much.

"I am. Wow, Logan said you were pretty, but he didn't tell me you're a knock-out."

I barely held back from rolling my eyes. "Thanks." I searched for a return compliment, but I came up empty. "So should we go in? I'm starved."

Travis grinned. "Sounds good. Me, too."

The nice thing about having a blind date at a restaurant was that the first fifteen minutes were taken up by being seated, the waiter taking our drink order—we both requested white wine—and the two of us examining the menu while we discussed options.

"Oh, their clams over linguine look good."

"Really?" I tried not to gag. "I'm not big on clams myself. I was looking at the chicken Parmesan. That's always a safe choice."

"You eat chicken?" There was a note of judgment in his voice. "I've been a vegetarian since I saw that movie about the practices of most poultry and beef farms."

I didn't know how to respond to that statement. If I claimed ignorance, I was afraid he'd tell me about the movie and I'd never be able to eat. If I said I was familiar with it, he'd think I was a heartless bitch who just wanted to eat, regardless of what had happened to her food before it reached her plate. It was a lose-lose situation.

Luckily for me, the waiter appeared at the table before I could choose the lesser of two evils. He set down our wine glasses and stood poised to take our order.

Travis inclined his head. "Ladies first."

Shit. Now I had to figure out something fast. "Ah, well, okay. I guess I'll have the capellini with tomatoes and basil." There, that was a safe choice, unless Travis had something to share about the cruel treatment of tomatoes during the harvest.

"And I'll have the clams over linguine." Travis handed our menus to the waiter, who hustled off to put in our order. Rubbing his hands together, my date beamed at me. "So, Emmy. Tell me about yourself. What are your hobbies?"

I frowned. "Hobbies? Well, honestly, I don't have a lot of free time in my life these days. I have a pie business that I run myself, and I work on weekend nights at the Riptide." I paused. "Did Logan tell you anything about me?"

He waved his hand. "Oh, yeah, he said something about you working at his wife's bar. That's nice. But you don't have anything you do just for fun? Or to keep in shape?"

"Not unless you count running my kids around." I pasted on a smile. "Logan did tell you I have three kids, right?"

"Yeah, he mentioned it. I like kids." Travis sipped his wine. "But my real passion is bicycling. I spend most of my non-working hours either training or doing races. I have an Orbea Orca Shimano." He sat back, looking at me expectantly.

"That's . . . great?" I honestly wasn't sure. It sounded a little like a terminal condition.

He frowned. "That's a top-of-the-line road bike. It's very expensive."

"Oh, okay." I fiddled with my napkin, curling the edges of it on my lap. "I don't know anything about bike racing."

"It's not hard to learn. I'd be happy to take you out some day, maybe on a ten-miler to start. Last month I did a run down to the Keys. It was beautiful."

"I'm sure." My head was beginning to pound, and I cursed past-Emmy who had ever thought that a blind date was a good idea. A convent sounded better. Being alone for the rest of my life sounded better than this. "Like I said, I don't have any free time. I'm either working or I'm with my kids. Usually I'm doing both at the same time. Or I'm sleeping, and I don't do enough of that."

"Oh." Travis seemed to get it, and he sat back, all enthusiasm gone. We sat in painful silence for a solid five minutes as the pain between my temples escalated.

"Jude said you're a lawyer. What kind of law do you practice?" I was scrambling for anything to end the enormous quiet.

"Mostly architect and engineering malpractice. I defend professionals who are being sued when something goes wrong in a building or a factory."

"Well, that sounds interesting." I was lying through my teeth. It sounded the opposite of interesting. It sounded more boring than watching paint dry.

"It isn't." Travis spoke flatly. "I only went to law school

because my father wouldn't get off my back. I wanted to be an activist, but he threatened to cut me off if I didn't go into a respectable line of practice."

At last. Something that made Travis a tiny bit likable. "Why don't you do that now? What's holding you back?"

He cocked his head. "What do you mean? I can't go back. I've got a solid practice built up now."

I nodded. "Sure, but why can't you sell it, take the money and go off to be an activist? What kind of work did you always want to do?"

Something flickered in his brown eyes. "I wanted to head up the places that protest animal cruelty and work to get laws passed that protect animals and require higher standards and practices for our food."

"You should totally go do it." I leaned forward. "I mean, why not? You're not married, right? You don't have kids. If you can afford a—what was it? An Orbi She-whatever? If you can buy that, you're probably making good money. You could live off it while you were getting yourself established in your new job. Your new life."

Travis stared at me as though I'd opened a door he'd never known existed. "I could. You know, I totally could." He slapped his hand down on the table, rattling the silverware and startling the older couple at the next table over. "Fuck my father. He doesn't control me anymore. Why didn't I think of this sooner?"

Well, you didn't think of it even now. I bit my tongue and smiled as the waiter brought our food.

The rest of the date was much more relaxed. Travis chattered with excitement about what he wanted to do with the rest of his life, and I did an excellent job of nodding and smiling. When the check came, Travis paid it and turned to me.

"Emmy, thanks. This was a turning point for me. I think if we hadn't gone out tonight, I never would've realized that I'm wasting my life."

I nodded, barely keeping a straight face. "I think you might be right, Travis."

"I'd like to say I could see you again, but I think I'm going to be pretty busy making over my life. And I think I'm going to get in touch with my girlfriend from college, too. The only reason we broke up was that she thought I was selling out. If I tell her I'm going back and making changes, maybe she'll reconsider."

I stood up and hitched my purse onto my shoulder. "Hope springs eternal, Travis." I offered him my hand. "Thank you for dinner. It was . . . enlightening."

As soon as I got back to the van, I called Jude and left a message on her voicemail. "Jude, it's Emmy. Don't tell Logan, but I think I broke his lawyer. Also, I think I'm over the whole blind-dating deal. I'll fill you in tomorrow."

Friday was another busy night at the Tide. I barely had a minute to give Jude the abbreviated version of my date report, but it turned out she'd already heard it; I'd talked to Abby on the phone that morning, and she'd spilled the beans to Jude.

"I can keep looking," she offered as she got ready to leave the restaurant. "There're plenty of other fish in the sea."

"I think I'm okay for now. I had an epiphany while I was with Travis. I like my life. I'm incredibly blessed. Maybe wanting to add a man to the mix is asking too much."

Jude's brows drew together. "Wanting to share your life with someone you love isn't asking too much, Emmy."

I shrugged. "If it happens, it happens. I'm not going to force anything." I patted her shoulder. "Don't worry, Jude. You did a good job. Travis seems like a decent person. Maybe I'm just not as ready as I thought I was." I tied the apron around my waist. "Now shoo. Don't you have a husband waiting at home for you?"

She nodded. "I'm sorry, though, Emmy. You deserve someone as wonderful as you are. Someone who can see how incredibly special you are." Before she turned to leave, she added, "It might take some people a while to see that. But don't give up on them. On love, I mean."

That thought stayed in the forefront of my mind as I ran myself ragged that night. We had to begin turning people away at about nine-thirty, and the dance floor stayed packed. But even as I filled drink orders, jumped in to bus tables and made sure everything ran smoothly, I realized I was keeping one eye open, looking for Cooper. I wanted to look up and see him sitting at the bar, his eyes searching me out.

I'd told him I couldn't handle casual sex, and I had a feeling he intended to take me at my word. He wouldn't show up here, hoping I might change my mind. That wasn't Cooper. He'd made his move, twice, and each time I'd responded. He wasn't going to push me when I'd said no to his proposed arrangement.

But if being with Travis had made me rethink dating, it

hadn't convinced me that I could live without sex for the rest of my life. As a matter of fact, being with Cooper twice had awakened something in me that had been dormant, and it wasn't likely to go back into hibernation. My body craved the touch of hands and lips, the sweet weight of a man on top of me, and I had a bad feeling that only one person would do.

The last customers left just before one. Carey and Aaron were exhausted, but they still stayed to help me close up. I sent everyone else home, calling goodnight as I made my rounds, checked to make sure the stoves and fryers were off and gave the restrooms a once-over. I thought of Cooper helping me with this last weekend, and a wave of intense longing swept over me, nearly pulling me under.

"Hey, Emmy. I just found a whole chocolate pie in the fridge." Aaron held up the dessert for me to see. "We can't serve it after tonight, since it was made Wednesday. Jude must've forgotten it was here."

"I brought her a few extras this week since we've been so busy." I looked at the delectable pie. "Do you or Carey want to take it home?"

Aaron shook his head. "I don't like chocolate."

I clapped my hand to my chest in mock horror. "Blasphemer! Okay, how about you, Carey?"

The girl ducked her head. "Thanks, but I'm not eating desserts. I'm trying to lose weight."

Aaron stared at her, his brows drawn together. "Why would you do that? You're not fat. You're perfect."

I bit back a smile that threatened as Carey's face pinked and blossomed into a smile. "Thanks."

"Well, if neither of you wants the pie, I guess I'll just . . ." I stopped talking as

an idea began to take shape in my mind. "I'll take care of it. I think I might know someone who'd enjoy it."

Aaron and Carey suddenly seemed in a hurry to leave, so I sent them out. I grabbed the pie and carried it with me as I finished closing up, set the alarm and locked the door. When I got into my van, I set the pie on the floor and turned the opposite direction from my house.

I hadn't actually ever been to Cooper's house. I knew where it was, because I'd dropped off Jude there a time or two to meet Logan. I knew from word around town that he'd bought the Cape Cod dirt-cheap and renovated both it and the huge workshop in the back; according to Jude, he had an apartment upstairs in the house, above his offices.

I pulled into the tree-shaded driveway, suddenly aware of just how late it was. It was nearly two in the morning, and Cooper was probably asleep. I was insane. What had made me think this was in any way a good idea? I could only blame sexual frustration. Need. Plain old horniness. God, I was pathetic.

A sound at the end of the driveway broke the stillness of the night. It came from the workshop, and I realized, with a mix of relief and giddy excitement, that there were lights on in that building. Cooper must be up, working.

Without taking any more time to second-guess myself, I slid out of the van, carrying the pie like an offering to the gods. The gravel and crushed shells crunched beneath my sneakered feet, and I was certain the sound echoed through the neighborhood. I tried to walk slower, more quietly.

There was a door at the end of the workshop, and when I turned the knob, it opened easily, surprising me. I took a deep breath and went inside.

For a moment, I thought I was alone. I was in a long room, filled with wood, furniture in various stages of completion and so many tools and machines. Sawdust scented the air, reminding me of Cooper's unique smell. My eyes wandered, taking in the different woods and the shelves of stain and paints, all in a kind of chaotic order that I assumed made sense to Coop.

A loud whining at the far end of the workshop pulled my attention in that direction, and I spotted Cooper, in jeans, with a white T-shirt stretched tight over his muscled back, standing at the disc sander. He wore goggles to protect his eyes, and his attention was wholly focused on the small piece of wood in his hand.

I stayed where I was, knowing that disturbing him when he was using the sander wasn't a good idea. At best he'd risk ruining the piece he was working on, and at worst, he could injure himself. I stood very still, waiting and watching.

It wasn't a hardship. His jeans were snug over his ass, reminding me all too vividly of what it felt like to cup my hands there. The muscles beneath his shirt shifted and rolled as he maneuvered the wood. I wanted to stand behind him, feather my fingers over his back and close my eyes as I felt him move. I wanted his hard body pressed against mine. I wanted him to surround me with his strength and never let go.

I wanted.

As though he could feel my desire, Cooper stepped back

from the sander, letting it slow to a stop. One hand swept off his goggles as he turned, his reaction at seeing me there barely discernable. He raked his fingers through his hair, brushing off the sawdust. And then he just stood, watching me, and waiting.

Licking my lips, I took one step forward. I wanted to be closer, yet part of me was still afraid. Still hesitating. I pushed that part of me down and took another two steps, lifting up my offering.

"I brought you pie."

Cooper's eyes flickered down to take note of the dessert. One side of his mouth lifted. "Looks good. Anything else?"

I took another step and another deep breath. I met his eyes, letting them take me captive into their bright blue electricity.

"I brought you . . . me."

Cooper blinked, once, and then he moved fast, like a cat. One hand took the pie plate, setting it on a nearby table, before he pulled me hard against him, his mouth open and over mine, his tongue sweeping possessively into me, stroking against my tongue and teeth. His hands gripped my ass, lifting me up until I wrapped my legs around his waist. With a grunt, he pushed a pile of wood off the workbench and settled me there.

He broke the kiss to lick his way down my neck, tugging down the collar of my shirt and pushing one breast free. He yanked down the bra cup and fastened his mouth on the turgid nipple, making me moan as I held his head close to me.

"I have to be inside you." His fingers were between my legs and hooked the thin cotton of my khaki shorts. He gave a hard jerk, and the cloth ripped. I almost sobbed with the overwhelming desire gripping me when he pushed aside the last barrier of my underwear. His fingers were rough and insistent, driving me up and up as I held tight to his shoulders.

Cooper removed his hand from me just long enough to undo his jeans, releasing his straining cock. He held it in one hand, pulling my backside closer to the edge of the bench with the other and thrusting into me without any hesitation.

I could feel the tightening low in my stomach, the undeniable sense that I was about to go flying over the edge into the abyss. I lifted my legs a little higher, changing the angle of our connection. Lying back, I rested on my elbows, throwing my boobs forward. Cooper growled and leaned down to suck on the exposed nipple before he moved to the other side, biting down through the layers of my shirt and bra.

The sting of pain and pleasure toppled me over the edge, my fingers digging into the wood of the bench as I arched my hips and cried out.

Cooper held my legs, but he never stopped plunging into me. When I dropped my head back, emptied by the strength of my orgasm, he gripped my hips harder.

"More. Give me more. Come again."

I gasped. "Don't think I can."

"Yes, you can. I want to feel you pulsing around my cock, Em. I'm so deep in you. So fucking deep. Can you feel me? I want to feel you come again, and I want your pussy to squeeze my dick."

The dirty words came tumbling from his mouth, turning me on again, and when he moved one hand to press against my clit, I screamed my pleasure. Cooper thrust one more time, hard enough to push my whole body backward, and came, spilling into me as endless spasms gripped my channel, squeezing him.

I hadn't quite caught my breath when Cooper lifted me again, holding me tight against his chest this time. He kissed my cheek and then my forehead.

"Hi, Emmy."

I giggled, unable to hold it back. "Hi, Coop."

"I'm glad you came over tonight. Glad you brought pie. Even gladder you brought you."

I nuzzled his neck, drawing circles with the tip of my tongue on his salty skin. "Me, too. Are you hungry? We can cut the pie."

He chuckled. "I could eat. I haven't had anything all day, and just now, I think I might've worked up an appetite."

I wriggled. "Then let me down, and we can take it inside. I assume you have a kitchen somewhere on the premises?"

Cooper tightened his hold on me. "I do have a kitchen. I have a coffeemaker, if you'd like coffee with your pie." He skimmed a light kiss over my lips. "I also have a bed. And I'm not going to put you down, because I've discovered that I'm kind of addicted to carrying you. I like feeling you against me, and I like having your mouth right here." He kissed me again, deeper and more involved this time.

"I can live with that." I breathed the words against his mouth as he headed for the door, stopping just long enough for me to snag the pie from the table before we slid into the night.

Chapter Eight

Cooper

I'D NEVER WOKEN UP WITH a woman in my bed.

It was true, I realized, as I opened my eyes. My hookups always took place elsewhere; either at hotels or at the girl's house. I'd bought this place while I was married to Jolie, but at the time, we'd lived in a small house closer to town. When I'd met Karlee, she'd never wanted to stay at what she termed my dingy little apartment; I had planned to build us a house, but the marriage hadn't lasted long enough for that. It had taken place entirely in a rented beachfront condo.

This morning, when I awoke to the sight of Emmy, still asleep with her hair spread over the pillow, lips slightly parted, something inside me shifted. She felt right here. I wanted to open my eyes and find her here all the time.

A tiny trace of chocolate was smeared on her bare shoulder, and I smiled. We'd enjoyed her chocolate pie last night. I'd convinced Emmy that we should eat it in bed, and when she dropped a little crumb onto her boob, I'd been lured into licking it off. That had led to more chocolate in more . . . interesting places, which had led to me coming hard in Emmy's seductive little mouth at the same time that she came against mine.

All of that chocolate meant that we needed to shower before we slept, and it only made sense to save water and shower together. Which had of course resulted in me taking her again, up against the wet tiles.

It had been nearly four before we fell asleep. I twisted to see my bedside clock, surprised that it was only ten now. I settled back down, drawing Emmy back against my chest.

"What time?" Her voice, sleepy and husky, was muffled against me.

"Ten." I traced circles on her arm. "You still tired? We didn't sleep long."

"Hmmm." She turned her head and kissed my arm. "I could wake up. For the right incentive."

I grinned. "I might be able to provide that." I threaded my fingers through her hair, sweeping it back from her face. "What's on your agenda for today?"

She lifted one shoulder, her eyes still closed. "Regular stuff. Nothing pressing. Nothing that can't be dealt with tomorrow. What about you?"

"Actually, I'm supposed to drive up to St. Augustine and pick up a dresser. Jude found it up there, and she wants it for the Hawthorne House. I'm going to restore it, so I told her I'd bring it down." I kissed Emmy's temple. "Come with me."

I half-expected her to refuse, but surprising me seemed

to be this woman's gift. "To St. Augustine? Oh, I'd love to." She turned in my arms, her face inches from mine. "It's one of my favorite places, and I never have time to go anymore."

I slid my hands between us, palming her breast and teasing one nipple with my thumb. "Sounds like a good plan then." I found her lips, kissing her slowly, with lazy sensuous touches. Her hands came up to frame my face, so soft and tender that I swore I melted into her.

We didn't speak as I raised myself over her and sank inch by slow inch into her body. When I was fully inside her, we were still, savoring the sensation of being connected. I could feel her breathing, the rise and fall of her lungs. I pressed against her, and she skimmed her fingers over my back. I moved once, lifting and then sliding back with deliberation. Emmy sucked in a breath, her breasts tantalizing my chest. I slipped one hand between us and found her, wet, slick and waiting. Still deep inside her, I stroked her clit with small, teasing touches until she gasped and arched, coming with silent intensity that pushed me into my own strong orgasm.

I fell onto her, my face buried in her neck while her hands soothed me and her lips rained small kisses on my hair.

This was peace, I realized. I felt . . . right. Content. If I died right there, in Emmy's arms, it would be with a smile on my face and my only regret that I didn't have one more moment with her.

"So where are we picking up this dresser?" Emmy propped her feet on the dashboard of my Jeep and glanced at me over the top of her sunglasses. I couldn't answer her right away, because I was pretty sure my heart had stopped. Sitting there in my passenger seat, her long legs on display and those gorgeous eyes looking at me . . . yeah, this chick had me. She was breathtaking. Insanely beautiful, in denim shorts (we'd stopped at her house for a change of clothes, since I'd ripped her other ones), a green T-shirt and flip -flops, with her hair down and curling over her shoulders.

"Uh . . ." I tried to remember her question. "Oh, yeah. The dresser. It's at an antique store on King Street. The guy's expecting me."

"Cool." She looked out at the ocean, her chest rising as she took a deep breath. "This is the prettiest drive, going up A1A. The weather's perfect, I'm riding in a Jeep . . ." She slid me a saucy look. " . . . with an okay-looking guy—"

"Okay-looking?" I poked her in the ribs, feigning insult. "Pretty sure that's not what you were saying around three this morning, when you were sucking chocolate off my—"

"Fine, fine, fine." Emmy reached one finger to trace my jaw. "Riding in a Jeep with a super-hot, handsome, sexy dude who did me ten ways to Sunday last night."

I laughed, trying to hide how her words affected me. Especially one particular part of me. "Much better."

"The only thing missing is music." She reached for the radio, pushing the power button and twirling the tuning knob until she found a station. "Here we go."

The music that floated out of my speakers was

undoubtedly country. It wasn't horrible, but I recognized the twangy voice and banjo.

"Uh-uh. Oh, no. Country music is not allowed in my Jeep." I reached to change the station.

Emmy pushed to sit up straight in her seat, crossing her arms over her chest and pushing out her bottom lip in an adorable pout. "What's wrong with country music?"

I flicked her cute little nose with the tip of my index finger. "You know I don't like country. You told me last weekend that you knew it."

"Well, yeah, but that was live at the restaurant. This is riding in the Jeep, alongside the beach, on a beautiful day with the sun shining and the wind blowing over us . . ." She trailed off and sighed, seeing that I wasn't going to give in. "Fine. What kind of music do you want?"

I hit a pre-tuned button on the radio. "Eighties music. Rock. You know, like Bon Jovi and Van Halen and Def Leppard." Drums filled the air as Jon Bon Jovi sang about being wanted.

Emmy wrinkled her nose. "Seriously? This is what you like?" She shook her head.

"Hey, you grew up in the same era. Don't knock it."

"Nuh uh, I'm four years younger than you. Our music was much better. Plus I always liked country."

I rolled my eyes. "How can you not like this? I thought all girls were hot for Jon Bon Jovi."

"Not this one. And Van Halen? All that hair?"

"Hey, hey. Don't knock Van Halen. A very important milestone in my life took place with them playing in the background."

Emmy turned to curl in her seat, tucking her legs under her as she smiled at me. "Oh, do tell. A very important . . . oh, my God. You lost your virginity to Van Halen?"

"That sounds wrong. No, I lost my virginity to Sheri Halwyn, while Van Halen was playing on the radio." I grinned, remembering. "It was *Panama*. That song still makes me hard."

"Gross. And Sheri Halwyn was a total slut." She shook her head, but I saw her lips twitching.

"She really was." I sighed, nostalgic. "But she liked Van Halen, too."

"Sheri liked *everyone*, as long they were male. The fact that she liked that music doesn't help your case."

"Oh, yeah? And what was playing when you gave it up, baby?"

Her smile faded. "Well, it wasn't country. Eddy hated it, too. It was *Sweet Love* by Anita Baker. Playing on a clock radio in a dingy little motel room up in Daytona. I didn't want my first time to be in a pickup truck, so we drove up there, and . . . yeah."

It was irrational and stupid, but my blood boiled at the thought of Eddy Carter taking her to a no-tell motel for her first time. I didn't even want to picture them together; it made me sick to my stomach, which I realized was completely stupid, since they'd been married and had three children. I didn't even know Emmy then. But I wanted to make up for it all now. I wanted to make every time we made love perfect and special, so she'd realize . . .

I pulled up my thoughts fast. *What the hell?* Where had all that come from? I didn't own Emmy, and I didn't owe her anything. We were . . . well, I wasn't sure what we were, but to-day we were together, riding along next to each other through this perfect day. I wasn't going to ruin it by overthinking every-thing. I was going to enjoy it, and to hell with consequences.

I reached across the console and snagged her hand, twin-ing our fingers together. I felt her surprise before she relaxed, tightening her grip.

For today, at least, she was mine, and I didn't need any-thing else.

"I don't think I can eat one more bite." Emmy leaned back, closing her eyes. "This was so good."

We were sitting on the patio at Harry's. Since it was after lunch and well before dinner, we were the only two customers still there. We'd already had our leftovers packed up and I'd paid the check.

I groaned. "I know. Me, neither. We'll have to come back another time to try their dessert. I've heard they make a mean bread pudding."

"I'm definitely up for that." Emmy pulled out her phone and glanced at the time. "We should probably start heading back. I need to go home and change before I go to the Tide."

"Yeah, I know." I stood up, stretching. "Don't worry, I'll get you home from the ball on time, Cinderella."

We walked back to the Jeep through the charm of Old Town, Emmy's hand secure in mine. We'd wandered here most of the day, window shopping and talking. I'd realized anew how much I enjoyed simply being with Emmy. She was easy, fun and interesting. I loved watching her face as she took in the old buildings and history.

The dresser was roped in, secured and ready for the ride to my workshop. When we reached the Jeep, I opened Emmy's door before jogging around to the driver's side.

We drove out of town, and Emmy sighed. I glanced over at her, noticing the little smile playing over her lips.

I lifted our joined hands to my mouth and kissed her fingers. "Did you have a good time today?"

"The best. I can't remember when I've enjoyed a day more." Her smile grew to involve her whole face. "Thank you, Cooper."

"Hey, it was fun for me, too. Thanks for coming with me." I waited a minute before asking her the question burning on my lips. "Can I come over tonight?"

She didn't reply right away, and my gut twisted. "I want you to. And I should just leave it at that. But I have to ask you, Coop. What're we doing?"

It was the same thing I'd been trying not to think about all day. "Does it matter, Em? Can't we just . . . be? Do we have to label it?"

Emmy twisted in her seat. "Maybe not. Maybe I'm just being a girl. What I said to you last week still holds. I'm not cut out for a sex-only deal. But clearly I like the sex. So I guess I'm just a hypocrite."

"Hey, I like your hypocrisy." I smirked, but when Emmy didn't respond, I got serious again. "I want more than just sex, too, Em. I wouldn't have asked you to spend today with me if I only wanted to sleep with you. I like you. I like spending time with you. But I still think I'm incapable of sustaining a real relationship. So can you give me a little time? Let's take things slow and see how they develop. Does that work for you?"

She nodded. "I guess so. I'm not asking for forever, Coop, and I don't expect perfection. But I need more than I have now. I can't go back to just working and sleeping. I've had a taste of what we could be together, and I want it."

I thought about the day we'd just spent together, how easy everything was with Emmy. I thought about waking with her next to me, her head on my pillow. I didn't want to go back to life without her, either. But I knew myself. I knew that I was capable of screwing up the best things in my life, and I couldn't do that to Emmy.

So I only held her hand a little tighter and drove on through the fading light.

Chapter Nine

Emmy

"EMMY, THANKS SO MUCH FOR coming in early." Jude met me at the entrance to the bar. She wore a pretty green skirt with a sleeveless blouse, and her hair, almost always up in a high ponytail, was down around her shoulders. I was so used to seeing her in shorts or jeans that seeing her dressed up took me by surprise.

"No problem at all. Mom's picking up the kids from school and taking them right home with her. A few extra hours don't hurt anyone." I went behind the bar and pulled on an apron.

"I appreciate it anyway. All this wedding stuff is getting intense. I found out about this meeting just this morning, and of course, Brenna's got a cold, so Lindsay has to stay home with her, and Joseph's got finals this week." Jude rolled her eyes. "You know, when Meggie said she wanted a simple beach wedding, very low-key, I figured I'd gotten off easy. I thought we'd throw some burgers on the grill here at the Tide, and all of us would just stand around in shorts while she and Sam got married. Ha!" She picked up her purse and dug around in it. "Now we've got a wedding planner, and musicians, and a tent . . . and we had to find a hotel to put up all the guests from Georgia." She sighed. "I wish we had the Riverside up and running. Just think how easy that would be."

"Is that a done deal?" I leaned on the bar, watching as Jude fussed with her lipstick. Cooper had told me about Jude and Logan' plans for the old hotel. I'd seen it, and while I'd seen my friends work miracles before, I had my doubts about the future of that ramshackle place.

"Yup. Closing's next week, and we're pushing through all the permits and variances. It'll be a while before it opens, of course, but I'm excited."

"So what wedding fun is on the agenda for today?"

"We're meeting with the wedding planner to go over the final schedule, the list of photographs, the music for the service . . . all the fun stuff. Meghan's joining us on video chat." Jude shook her finger at me. "Here's a word of wisdom for you. When it's time for Izzy and Dee to get married, make sure they don't expect you to do all the legwork while they're three hours away."

I laughed. "Jude Hawthorne Holt, you're so full of it. You love this. And you wouldn't have it any other way."

Jude snorted and then laughed, too. "Okay, you're right. I am loving it. I do wish Meggie were a little closer, though. I keep remembering how much fun my mom and I had

planning my wedding, and I feel like most of my conversa-
tions with Meghan are over text or video chat. I miss her."

I thought of the pretty young girl who I'd watched grow
up. "I can imagine. But she seems awfully happy."

"She really is. I never thought she'd end up a farmer's
wife, but she loves Burton, and she loves the farm. And most
important, she loves Sam, and he loves her. He's a wonderful
guy."

"I've liked him each time I've met him. His friend Alex
is a hoot, too. I'm looking forward to seeing him again at the
wedding."

Jude smiled. "Me, too. Logan and I have been thinking . . .
well, I better not say anything about it yet. We need to finalize
a few things first."

"You're such a tease." I stuck out my tongue at her. "Now
get out of here before the wedding planner and Meghan cook
up more things for you to do before the wedding. I'm fine
here, and I'll see you tomorrow afternoon."

"Thanks, sweetie. Be careful, have a good night. Make
lots of money."

The restaurant was quiet once Jude left. I wasn't used to
being there at that time of the day by myself. I'd covered daytime hours before now and then, but usually Sadie and Mack,
the older couple who'd been working at the Tide since time
eternal, were there with me. And of course, since Joseph and
Lindsay moved home and took over part of the restaurant's
operations, one of them was usually on the premises.

I took advantage of the lull to check on our supplies for
the night ahead. Carey and Aaron would be showing up soon

to take over the cooking, but for now, if anyone came in to order food, it was on me. I scraped one of the grills, even though it really didn't need it. Jude had cleaned up from the lunch run, and the kitchen was in good order. I decided to cut some fries, since it was a given that someone would come in and order those at some point in the next hour.

I'd just finished my third potato when I heard the bell over the door ring. "Be right with you! Have a seat anywhere." I washed and dried my hands as I came out of the kitchen section to the bar.

At first, I didn't see anyone in the dining room. And then I spotted her. Lexie Davis stood just inside the door, glancing around nervously. She was twisting her hands as she shifted from foot to foot.

"Hey, Lex. This is a surprise."

At the sound of my voice, she jerked her head in my direction, and I realized her eyes were red and swollen. My heart dropped as the worst scenario possible flew through my head. *Cooper. Something happened to Cooper.*

It didn't take me long to realize how stupid that was. If something had happened to Coop, Jude would've known. Plus, he'd sent me one of his rare texts that afternoon, just before I left home to drive to the Tide.

See you tonight. I'll be at the bar until closing.

It was the closest Cooper came to making plans with me, but it made me smile, because I knew he hated sending texts. Things between us had been calm the last few weeks. I realized that was because I wasn't pushing any issues, which relieved Cooper. I was letting him have his way for now, taking things slowly. The only problem was that slowly seemed to be where we were doomed to stay. I had a mental image of us in rocking chairs, with Cooper telling me not to rush him into anything.

I gave myself a mental shake. Here was his daughter standing at the door, obviously in distress, and I was staring off into space, fantasizing about her father. *Nice, Emmy.*

"Lexie, what's wrong, sweetheart?" I came out from the bar and met her halfway across the restaurant.

"Oh, Emmy. I'm glad it's you here." She launched herself at me, and I folded her into a hug. Her thin shoulders shook as she wept against me. "I—" She hiccoughed, trying to speak. "I love Aunt Jude, but you'll understand more. I can talk to you."

That was gratifying. Lexie and I had hit it off the last two summers when she'd worked at the Tide. I was glad she felt she could trust me. "What's going on, Lex? Are you okay?"

She shook her head. "I'm such a loser, Emmy. And he said I was acting like a kid. And then he slept with Kaley, and she's such a slut." She covered her eyes with one hand, tears pouring over her fingers.

I steered Lexie to a chair and sat down across the table from her. "Okay, honey, I think you need to start from the beginning. First things first. Does your mom know you're in the Cove? Or your dad?"

Lexie dropped her eyes to the floor. "Noooo. Not exactly. Mom and Alton had to go to a big dinner tonight in Jacksonville, so I was supposed to go right home and heat up leftovers. But then Bryan and I had a huge fight, and so

I called a cab and came here. I wanted to see Daddy. But he wasn't at home, and I didn't want to call him and have him freak out. I thought he might be here."

"He had a dentist appointment this afternoon. That's probably where he was." I spoke without thinking how odd it might seem to Lexie that I knew when her father was going to the dentist. And actually, I only knew it because he'd groused to me last weekend about how much he hated the dentist. Since his appointment was on a Friday afternoon, I'd promised him a very special treat if he behaved himself during his cleaning. Of course, that wasn't something I could share with his daughter.

Lexie frowned, her eyes narrowing. "How did you know that?"

I forced a laugh. "Oh, Lex, you know the Cove. Everyone knows everything about each other. Your father was whining about having to go when I saw him last weekend, here at the Tide, and I called him a baby. Men." I rolled my eyes.

To my relief, she relaxed. "He's totally a baby about the dentist, you're right. Mom always says I handle it better than Daddy does."

"I'm sure she's right. Speaking of your mom, let's call her now and tell her where you are, and then you can tell me what happened with Bryan."

Lexie made a face, wrinkling her forehead. "Do I have to call her? She's going to freak out, and I don't think I can handle her right now." Tears pooled in those blue eyes, so like her father's. I sighed.

"Okay, Lex. Give me her number, and I'll call."

She smiled and leaned across the table. "Thank you, Emmy! I love you." She dug her phone from her back pocket and scrolled through until she found her mother's contact info. I typed it into my phone and waited for Jolie to pick up.

"Hello?" Her voice was cautious, curious, probably wondering who was calling her from an unfamiliar number.

"Hi, Jolie? This is Emmy Carter, from Crystal Cove."

"Oh, of course." Jolie's voice still held traces of North Carolina. "What can I do for you, Emmy? Everything okay?" The caution had left, but the curiosity was still there.

"Well, I just wanted to let you know I've got Lexie here with me. She's fine, don't worry, but I guess she's had some—some upset, and she came down to the Cove to see Cooper, but she couldn't find him so she came down here to the Tide. She's sitting with me. I thought you'd want to know."

"Oh, my God. How did she get down there?" Jolie sounded equal parts pissed and upset. I didn't exactly blame her.

"She took a cab."

"A *cab*? All the way from Daytona to the Cove? And just how did little miss thing pay for this cab?"

I was beginning to feel like calling Jolie had been a bad idea. "Uh, I don't know. I didn't ask her." I held the phone away from my ear. "Lex, your mom wants to know how you paid for the cab."

She ducked her head. "I used her credit card that she gave me for emergencies."

My eyes went wide, but I put the phone back to my ear. "Jolie, she says—"

"I heard what she said. Good God, that had to have been—I don't even want to think how much it was." She blew out a long breath. "I'm sorry to put you in the middle of this, Emmy. Will she talk to me?"

Lexie shook her head violently. I gave her my stern mom face, but apparently it only worked on my own children, because she backed away from me.

"Jolie, I'm sorry, but she's pretty upset. I don't know exactly why yet. We were going to address that after I called you."

Jolie sighed. There seemed to be a lot of that going around. "All right. Did you call Cooper?"

"Uh, not yet. I'm not sure he's back from the dentist."

If Jolie also thought it was odd that I'd know that kind of information about her ex-husband, she didn't let on. "I'll call him and let him know he needs to get his ass down there to get his daughter. She can stay all weekend with him, and maybe he can straighten her out."

If it was shallow and petty that my heart sank at that idea—Lexie staying with Cooper all weekend meant I wouldn't get to see him—then I was shallow and petty.

"Okay, well—just tell him she's fine here until he can come over."

"I will. And thank you, Emmy, for thinking to call me. I appreciate it." The click indicated that our call was over, and I raised one eyebrow as I set down my phone.

"She's really mad, isn't she?" Lexie bit her lip.

"I wouldn't say she's pleased." I sat back in my chair and folded my arms over my chest. "Okay, Lex. Spill. What happened today?"

She swallowed and fastened her eyes on the table, where her fingers traced a line in the grain. "My boyfriend Bryan— we've been going out three months. And he's so cool. So cute. And everyone likes him, and I never thought he'd ask *me* out, because he doesn't date younger girls, but he did, even though he's a senior and I'm a sophomore."

"He sounds very nice." No, actually, he didn't, but I was going to reserve judgment until I had the full story.

"He's been wanting to—to go all the way. Hook up. All our friends do, he says, and I just can't because my mom is so strict. I'm not allowed to stay out late or spend the night at the beach or anything. So when I told him that Mom and Alton were going to Jacksonville tonight for this dinner, he said it was our chance. He was going to come over and we were going to do it."

I nodded, but my mind was reeling. *Cooper's going to kill this boy. He's going to shoot him. Oh my God, what am I going to do?*

"But at the last minute, I chickened out. I told him I couldn't do it, I wasn't ready. I want to be ready, but I'm just not."

"That's a very mature decision, Lexie." I reached across the table and laid my hand over hers. "I'm proud of you."

"Thanks." Tears spilled out down her cheeks. "But Bryan said I'm acting like a baby. He said all his friends make fun of him for dating a sophomore, but he thought I was mature for my age, and now I'd proved him wrong and made him look like an idiot. He was so mad, Emmy. I was almost afraid of him."

My blood ran cold. *Okay, forget about Cooper. I'm going to kill this kid.*

"And while he was yelling at me, he told me he'd been sleeping with Kaley. My best friend Kaley. We've been friends since kindergarten, and she's been screwing him all along." Lexie broke into sobs again, laying her head down on her folded arms.

I stroked her hair, feeling helpless. "Oh, honey. I'm so sorry. Are you sure he's not lying about Kaley, just to get you to . . . well, to get his way?"

She shook her head. "I called Kaley and she admitted it. She said it didn't mean anything, it was just hooking up, but it means something to me."

"Of course it does. Oh, Lex, I'm so sorry. I'm sorry you've had your heart broken by someone who never deserved to have it in the first place."

She lifted her tear-streaked face. "I hate love. I never want to fall in love again in my life. I suck at it. I'm such a loser."

"Baby girl, you're not." I scooted my chair around next to her so I could hold her. "Lexie, right now it feels like the world's ending, and I understand that. Believe me, honey, I do. And you never want to feel this way again. It hurts so much, it would be easier to just protect your heart and never let it risk hurting."

She nodded, heaving sobs shaking her body.

"I get it. I've been there. But you can't feel that way. Because someday, someone's going to come along who's actually worthy of this beautiful heart of yours. And when he does, you're going to realize that all the other morons who came before meant nothing to you. You'll know what love really is. Love doesn't intentionally hurt the other heart. Real love would do anything to make the other heart happy, to protect it. And that's what you're going to find someday."

Lex sniffled, pulling a napkin from the dispenser to wipe her nose. "When your husband left you, did it feel like this?"

I hesitated. "It hurt, yeah. It was hard. But you know why? Because I'd wasted way too many years with someone who didn't really love me. And I realized that I hadn't loved him for a long time. We had a high school love, and sometimes those are real and true, like with Jude and Daniel. But lots of times they aren't. By the time I realized that Eddy wasn't my love, I already had kids, and I would do anything to protect my children, just like your mom and dad would for you."

Lexie breathed in deeply and let out a long breath. "Do you think you'll ever find someone else to love? Like, a real love?"

I thought of Cooper, holding my hand as we drove along the beach drive, carrying me to his bed, helping me close the Tide every week. Listening to me talk about my plans and dreams, encouraging me. Making me feel beautiful every time he looked at me.

"I think maybe I have."

"And does he love you, too?"

That was a harder question. If I thought about it too long, I'd end up sobbing here right alongside Lexie. "I don't know, honey. Sometimes love's funny that way. We might find the one person our heart wants, but it turns out that person can't love us, not the way we need him to. It doesn't mean our love is any less real. Then we have to decide if our love is strong enough for both of us."

"Do you think yours is?"

"I hope so. I hope—things work out. Because right now, I don't think I can stop loving him, even if he tells me he can't feel the same way." I shook my head. "But we're talking about you, not about me. This guy, Lex, he's a jerk. He's not worth one of your tears, and before long, you're going to realize how much better you are than either Bryan or your friend Kaley. Trust me."

Lexie nodded, though I wasn't sure she was entirely convinced. The door from the deck banged closed, and Cooper came into the restaurant.

He glanced at me, but I couldn't read his expression. His eyes skittered over to Lexie and softened.

"Oh, Daddy." She burst into tears again and leaped into her father's arms. I pushed my chair back to stand up.

"Alexis, don't you ever do anything like this again, do you hear me?" Cooper hugged her close and then held her at arm's length to look into her face. "Do you know how dangerous that was? A cab all the way from Daytona? You call me, and I'll come get you. I've told you that over and over."

"Let her tell you the story, Cooper. It's a little more complicated." I patted his shoulder as I passed them, and Cooper caught my hand before I could get away. He gazed at me, his eyes searching my face, but again I couldn't tell exactly what he was feeling. He mouthed the words *thank you* before releasing my hand.

Lexie had lifted her face from her father's chest, and

when I looked down at her, I realized she'd been watching me. Confusion clouded her eyes. Before she could ask any questions, I smiled and walked to the bar.

"Why don't you guys go sit on the deck to talk? I'll bring you some sweet tea. Except for you, Cooper. You have clean teeth, so you get water." I winked at Lexie.

Cooper tucked his daughter beneath his arm and steered her toward the door. "Thanks, Em. I appreciate it."

Once they were out of sight, I leaned against the bar, suddenly exhausted. My heart hurt for Lexie, for her first betrayal and lost love. And it hurt for me, too. Because I was pretty sure Cooper was the love of my life, the one man I'd never get over. And I wasn't sure I was strong enough to survive that kind of pain, if he decided he couldn't risk loving me back.

I laid my head down on the bar, wishing I could sob like Lexie had. But tears didn't come, and I was left with a hollow ache of dread.

∝⊙

Cooper

It was late on Sunday night by the time I headed back to the Cove from Daytona. Lexie had stayed with me all weekend, and we'd had hours of discussion about boys, love and heartbreak. It was the first time that I felt totally inadequate as a father. Up until now, I had been able to protect Lexie from most of life's hurts, at least the major ones. But now I could only listen and advise, knowing that I couldn't change how that dickhead and her so-called best friend had broken her heart.

I was proud of her, though and I told her that. She'd made the right decision, and even though Jolie was mad about the cab ride from Daytona—and I wasn't too thrilled about it, either—Lexie had done the best she could under the circumstances. When I talked to Jolie privately on the phone, I told her I thought getting out of town might've been a better choice than any of us knew.

"That jerkwad knew Lex was going to be home alone most of the evening. Who's to say he wouldn't have come over and attacked her while you were in Jacksonville?"

"Oh, Cooper, now I think you're making mad leaps to conclusions. I've met Bryan. He's a little cocky, sure, but what high school senior boy isn't? He seemed like a decent kid. I never would've let Lexie go out with him if I'd thought otherwise."

"Yeah, and we saw how well that worked out, didn't we?" I muttered. I still hadn't abandoned the plan to jump this kid in a dark alley and give him back a little of the hurt he'd inflicted on my little girl.

"Thanks, Coop, for that vote of confidence. Like you would've been able to tell the difference, either. Teenage boys don't come with their shortcomings stamped on their foreheads. If they did, most of them would go around with the words 'idiot' and 'horndog' on their faces." Her voice softened. "Besides, you can't protect her forever. She's growing up, and she's going to get hurt. She's going to fall in love, and her heart's going to get broken. Again. All we can do is to be there for her, to help her pick up the pieces."

"Hmmm." I rubbed my forehead. "I don't like it."

Jolie laughed. "You may not like it, buddy, but that doesn't make it less true." She paused, and I sensed I wasn't going to like what came next, either. "Speaking of love and broken hearts, Cooper, what's going on with you and Emmy Carter?"

I was struck speechless for a minute. I even strongly considered hanging up and claiming the call had been dropped. Finally I answered her.

"I don't know what you're talking about."

"Don't bullshit me, Cooper Davis. I've known you too long. I heard something in her voice when she called about Lexie. That was awfully sweet of her, by the way, to take care of Lex the way she did. I really appreciate it. I was so mad on Friday I'm not sure I told Emmy that. Pass it on for me, will you?"

"Sure, if I see her." I kept my tone careless.

"Whatever. Just try not to screw it up, okay? She seems like a really decent person. She'd be good for you."

"I'm not looking for someone to be good for me, Jolie. That ship sailed a long time ago."

"Yeah, yeah, yeah. Oh, by the way, while I have you on here, I wanted to tell you that Alton and I are getting married."

I nearly dropped the phone again. "What? Why? I thought you said you never wanted to be married again."

"I did say that, and I meant it at the time. And now I've changed my mind. Alton's wanted to be married for a long time, you know, and he said to me a few weeks ago that I should know by now he's not going anywhere, married or not, and so why shouldn't we make it official? I couldn't think of any reason to say no."

"Huh. Well, congratulations, I guess."

"Try to quell your excitement, Coop. You're going to make me cry." Jolie hesitated. "It took me a long time to get over what happened between you and me, you know. Which is silly, because it wasn't anything either of us did wrong. We just weren't cut out to be together. But I hope you don't have some crazy idea that you were to blame for everything."

"I'm not made for marriage, Jolie. I screw it up."

"Oh, for God's sake, Cooper. Stop being ridiculous. You were married to me when we were both children, basically, and then you were married to the nutcase. Neither of those are a compelling case for or against your ability to handle marriage. Now our wedding is going to be in September, at St. Luke's up here. I want you to be there. It's going to be very elegant and grown up. And bring Emmy."

I growled something about her biting me and hung up to the sound of her laughter.

It was too late to see Emmy by the time I got back to the Cove. I knew Sunday nights were busy for her, getting the kids ready for the next week of school and settling them back at home after their weekend at the grandparents' house. I considered texting her, just to let her know I was home and thinking of her, but I didn't actually do it. I hadn't seen her all weekend, not since Lexie and I had left the Tide on Friday afternoon. She knew I'd be occupied with my daughter, and she'd understand why I didn't show up Saturday night at the Tide. At least, I hoped she did.

But more than that was weighing heavy on me as I tromped from the Jeep to my workshop. On Friday, I'd just been getting back to the house from the damn dentist when my cell phone started buzzing. As soon as I'd gotten the basic story of Lexie's adventures from Jolie, I jumped back into the Jeep and headed for the Tide. Once I was parked, I went up through the deck, as I usually did. I opened the screen door that led into the bar, but before it slammed shut behind me, I heard Lexie's voice. And Emmy's. I froze, not wanting them to know I was there.

"Do you think you'll ever find someone else to love? Like, a real love?" Lexie was speaking, and I frowned, wondering who she was questioning.

There was a long silence, and then I recognized Emmy's voice. She sounded . . . sad.

"I think maybe I have."

"And does he love you, too?"

I strained my ears to hear how Emmy would answer this. Did she know how I felt? Did I want her to know it, or would it be easier if she just assumed I didn't care the same way she did?

"I don't know, honey. Sometimes love's funny that way. We might find the one person our heart wants, but it turns out that person can't love us, not the way we need him to. It doesn't mean our love is any less real. Then we have to decide if our love is strong enough for both of us."

I closed my eyes. God, she shattered me. Emmy, with all

her crazy strength, with everything she'd gotten through—what kind of asshole was I, making her think I couldn't love her?

"*Do you think yours is?*" My daughter wanted to believe. I could hear it in her tone.

"*I hope so. I hope—things work out. Because right now, I don't think I can stop loving him, even if he tells me he can't feel the same way.*"

I had to hold myself back from rushing into the restaurant, taking Emmy into my arms and kissing her until she knew that I'd lied to her. The idea that I didn't—or couldn't—love her was a huge lie, because it was obvious that I did. The only thing that stopped me from falling at her feet and telling her the truth was my daughter sitting there.

Emmy changed the subject abruptly, and I knew I had to get inside before I overheard more that I shouldn't. When I walked in and saw the two of them sitting there together, Emmy's arms wrapped around my daughter, I fell a little deeper in love.

I loved Emmy Carter. I was in love with her. She was beautiful, sexy and smart—but even more important, she was kind, compassionate and had the biggest heart I'd ever known.

But I had to figure out for myself what would be the kindest thing: letting myself love Emmy, or protecting her from the walking disaster that was my heart by hiding how I felt?

I wrestled with the question most of Sunday night as I tossed and turned and all of Monday, as I worked on various projects. I'd gone over with Logan and Jude to see the Riverside a few weeks back, and now that it was definitely theirs, I was working up estimates on the work they wanted me to do. I was convinced they were insane to tackle this one, but hey, who was I to judge? I couldn't even decide if I were healthy enough to love someone.

By dinnertime on Monday, I was restless and frustrated. I tossed down the pencil I'd been using to sketch out some of my ideas for the Riverside, grabbed my keys and stalked out to the Jeep. Without stopping to consider anything or anyone, I drove to Emmy's house.

I pulled in behind her ancient red minivan, set the parking brake on the Jeep and climbed out. At the front door, I hit the doorbell and waited, musing that I'd never had to knock at Emmy's door before. She was always with me to let me inside.

The door flew open, and a young girl with a long red braid stood there, frowning at me. After a minute, her expression cleared.

"Oh, hey, Mr. Cooper. Mom, it's Mr. Cooper!" Izzy yelled over her shoulder.

Emmy came into the living room, drying her hands on a dishtowel. Her eyes were wide in surprise.

"Hey, Coop. Did I miss something? Did we have an . . . uh, appointment?" Her face was flushed, and she glanced at her kids, as though she was afraid I was going to toss her down and have my way with her right there in front of them.

"No. Sorry for dropping by without calling, but I just needed to see you." It was the truth. I'd needed to see her the way an alcoholic needs the taste of whiskey trickling down his throat. Just being here with her gave me a measure of the peace I'd been missing all weekend.

"Well, we're about to get started on dinner. Want to stay?" My own longing was mirrored on her face.

"You should say yes." The boy who was sitting at the kitchen table looked around the doorway at me. "We're having fried chicken, and Mom makes the best. Plus biscuits."

I winked at Emmy. "You had me at fried chicken. Thanks, I'd love to stay. But only if I can help."

A small girl with blonde hair that was nearly white latched onto my hand and dragged me toward the kitchen. "You can help me set the table. That's my job."

"Dee, Mr. Cooper's a guest. He doesn't have to do anything at all." Izzy scolded her little sister and then glanced up at me. "Mr. Cooper, do you want something to drink?"

I caught Emmy's eye, smiling at her over the kids' heads. "I would absolutely love a drink, Izzy. How about lemonade?" I remembered Emmy telling me her oldest daughter had recently developed a passion for making it from scratch. My memory was rewarded when the girl's face lit up.

"Sure! Come sit down at the table. I'll get it for you." I followed her in and sat down next to Cameron, who was concentrating hard on a book and papers spread out over the table.

"Mom, I don't get this part. About the angles. I don't even know why I have to know this anyway." Cam tossed down the plastic protractor and scowled.

Emmy began to speak, but I interrupted. "Cam, do you

mind if I have a look? I might be able to help, and that way your mom can get going on that fried chicken for us."

Cameron nodded. "Yeah." He pushed the book toward me. "It's the part about measuring angles."

I checked out the lesson and smiled. "Well, you're in luck, Cameron, because this happens to be something I use every single day."

"You do?" The boy looked dubious.

I nodded. "Yup. I make furniture, you know, and other stuff for houses out of wood. I have to measure everything really carefully before I cut it, or it won't fit together. And the angles have to be perfect, or the wood could split when I put it together."

Cam looked interested. "So this isn't just crap they make us do in school? It's, like, real stuff?"

I bit back a laugh. "Yeah, it's real stuff. Now let me show you the best way to do this."

By the time Emmy was setting the chicken on the table, Cam was finished with his homework and telling me enthusiastically about the latest penny boards down at Matt's shop. I'd helped Dee set the table and drunk two glasses of Izzy's lemonade. All in all, I felt like it was a successful hour.

Dinnertime was a noisy and boisterous affair in the Carter house. The kids all chattered, tell Emmy about their day and adventures. Emmy asked questions, laughed at their jokes and made sure everyone ate. I watched them, thinking of my years of silent, lonely dinners, often standing at the workbench.

As soon as the last piece of chicken was finished and the

final biscuit argued over (Izzy won it), Emmy announced it was time for baths.

"Don't we have to help clean up?" Izzy glanced at her mother in surprise.

"Not tonight. You get a reprieve. Go get ready for a bath and lay out your clothes for tomorrow. And help your sister." When the kitchen was empty except for us and the noise had moved down the hall, Emmy looked at me, her eyes worried.

"I'm sorry about that. Three can be a lot, when you're not used to them. They're good kids, but they need my attention this time of night."

"Emmy." I touched her hand where it lay on the table. "This was the nicest dinner I've had in a long time. Please don't apologize for your kids. They're fantastic."

She smiled. "Well, I think so, but I'm a tad biased. It just struck me that you've only really known me as grown-up, child-free Emmy, not the me who's a mom." She spread her hands. "This is the whole package. I know it's a lot. And I know it's overwhelming."

"It's a pretty amazing package." I slid her hand into mine. "Emmy, I don't know what's going to happen with us, but no matter what, it won't have anything to do with your kids. They're part of you, and I admire the hell out of you for the job you're doing with them."

She dropped her gaze to the table. "Thanks, Cooper. I appreciate that." She cleared her throat. "So how's Lex doing?"

I shrugged. "Oh, she's going to live. Apparently her friend spent the weekend begging Lexie's forgiveness. I doubt they'll ever be friends again, but she'll probably forgive her. And the boy . . . if he knows what's good for him, he'll stay the hell away from my daughter."

Emmy nodded. "I wanted to break his neck." She spoke so matter-of-factly that I almost fell out of my chair. And then I laughed.

"Emmy Carter, one thing no one can say about you is that you're predictable." I stood up. "I better get going so you can put the kids to bed and have a little peace and quiet."

She looked up at me through her eyelashes. "You could stay, for a little while at least. Once they go to sleep, my peace and quiet could get a bit lonely."

I groaned. "Don't tempt me, woman. I have a few things to get done tonight. But I'll see you this weekend?"

"I'll be at the Tide Friday and Saturday. I can always use help closing up."

"Count on it." I glanced up the hallway and chanced dropping a quick kiss on her upturned face. "Thanks again for dinner."

Leaving the small house was harder than I'd expected. There was so much more home there than at my house. It was another piece of the Emmy puzzle, a picture that was becoming harder and harder to resist.

I drove aimlessly for the better part of an hour, cruising familiar spots. I drove past Daniel and Jude's old house, the one Logan had designed for her and Daniel had built. The two men had loved the same woman for over twenty years, though only one of them knew it. Daniel had been gone for nearly four years now, and his son Joseph lived in the house now with his wife Lindsay and their two kids. It was as it should be, and yet . . . I missed the days when I could drop in to sit by the pool and have a beer with Daniel.

Next I went by the Tide, closed up for the night. Matt's shop was dark, too; I imagined he was at home with Sandra and her daughter, possibly going through the same kind of routine I'd just seen at Emmy's house.

I drove down the beach line for a few miles and pulled into a familiar driveway. When I rang the doorbell, this time there was no red-haired child answering the door. Instead Logan swung it open, yawning as he stood aside.

"Cooper. This is a surprise. Come on in." He opened the door wider and I followed him into the great room. The house was quiet, and I glanced into the kitchen.

"Jude's out with Meghan. The bride just arrived today from Georgia." Logan chuckled. "They're out picking up favor bags, which apparently is something every wedding needs, even though I have no idea what the hell they are. Anyway." He pointed to the fridge. "Beer?"

"Wouldn't say no."

He pulled two bottles out and popped the lids for us. "Want to take them out on the deck? It's a nice night."

"Sure."

We settled into chairs, and Logan lifted his bottle toward mine. "To old friends. To the posse." It was our regular toast, and I clinked my bottle with his.

"So is the wedding stuff getting crazy?" I stared out at the ocean.

"Definitely, but Jude's having a blast, so I'm cool with it.

I think it's going to be good. They're all excited. Lindsay's got the cutest little outfits for the kids."

I shook my head. "Sometimes it blows my mind to think you and Jude are grandparents. Doesn't seem possible."

Logan shrugged. "Well, technically it's Jude who's a grand-mother. And she was a young mom, and Joseph's a young dad, so it's not that bad." He grinned. "I get to be PopPop Logan. I never thought I'd be that. So no complaints here."

"Was it hard, taking on a ready-made family?" I traced a drop of condensation down the side of my bottle.

Logan glanced at me curiously. "No. Because they belong to Jude. They're part of her, and I love her. And now they're part of me, too. Of course, Meggie and Joseph were pretty much grown when I came into the picture, but it wouldn't have made any difference. I wouldn't have cared if she had ten kids. I wanted the whole package."

I nodded, thinking that I'd used that same phrase earlier with Emmy. *The whole package.* Did I want that?

"So are you going to tell me what's up, or are you going to make me pull it out of you?" Logan propped his feet on the ottoman.

I sighed. "I think . . . I might be interested in someone."

"Uh huh."

"That's all you have to say?"

Logan laughed. "I was waiting for some elaboration be-fore I dispensed advice."

I rolled my eyes. "I'd think that'd be enough to make you sit up and take notice. Me, Cooper the love loser, actually con-sidering taking the plunge again?"

"Wait a second." Logan leaned forward. "Take the plunge? Are you really thinking about getting married again?"

I shook my head. "That's not quite on the table. I just mean, a relationship. A girlfriend. One woman. Exclusive."

"Yeah, so?"

"So you're supposed to talk me out of it. Remind me how I screw this shit up. How I shouldn't ruin someone else's life."

Logan frowned. "Cooper, who ever said you screw up relationships? Where's this coming from?"

"It's coming from two failed marriages, dude." I took another long swig of my beer.

"Yeah, well, you didn't have the best material to work with. Nothing against Jolie, but you guys got married too fast. And Karlee—" He cast me a look. "We all knew what was going down there. Everyone but you, anyway. But this isn't the same thing. Emmy's a great girl. She's smart, she's funny, she's sensible—"

"Hold on. Who said anything about Emmy?" I drew my eyebrows together.

"Oh, shit." Guilt colored Logan's face. "Well, we're talking about her, aren't we?"

I sighed in defeat. "Yeah, we are. How did you know?"

Logan closed his eyes and shook his head. "My wife. Jude and I went over to Emmy's one Saturday morning a few months back. Jude needed to drop something off. And your Jeep was in the driveway. We put two and two together . . ." He grimaced. "That's why Jude invited you and Abby over

191

here together that one night. She figured if it looked like we were match-making, you might come clean about Emmy."

"That wasn't very nice to Abby." I threw up my hands. "What the hell, Logan?"

"Abby knew. She told Emmy about it the next day, hoping to push her into admitting what was going on. The two of you are the most stubborn people I've ever known."

"We're not stubborn, Logan. We're private. Emmy and I . . . we don't know yet what's going on. We're taking it slow."

"Yeah. Good luck with that." Logan smirked.

"What's that supposed to mean?"

"It means everyone else in the world can see you're head over heels in love with Emmy, and she feels the same way about you. I don't know why the two of you don't just admit it and date like normal people."

"Because I don't want to do that to her, Logan. God, can't you see I wouldn't hurt Emmy for the world? And I'll end up doing it. I know I will."

"Yeah, you will. And she'll hurt you, too. It's part of being in love. Part of being together. And you'll make it up together, and life will go on. You don't throw away a chance at happiness because you're afraid of it, Cooper. I get that you've been burned before, but that's all the more reason to grab your chance now and run." He finished his beer and elbowed me. "You're not getting any younger, man. Emmy may be your last shot before you hit the nursing home."

"Nice, Logan. I come here for advice and I get insults."

"Hey, you got the advice, too. It's a package deal."

"Yeah, thanks." I stood up, tossing my empty into a

barrel Logan kept on the edge of the deck just for that purpose. "I'm heading home now. Thanks for the beer. And the insults."

"And the advice?" Logan grinned up at me from his chair.

"Not sure yet. Jury's still out. 'Night, Logan."

Chapter Ten

Emmy

THE DAY OF MEGHAN AND Sam's wedding dawned with such a clear blue sky that I wanted to cry. I lay in bed, looking out the window and remembering my own disastrous wedding fifteen years before. God, I'd been stupid.

I heard Dee's voice coming from the kitchen and smiled. Of course, if I hadn't been so stupid, I wouldn't have my three greatest blessings, and I didn't want to imagine life without my kids. No matter how much Eddy exasperated me, he'd given me three perfect gifts.

It was nice to have my kids at home on a Saturday morning, I thought. Jude had broken with every sort of tradition and closed the Tide for the entire weekend, even though the wedding wasn't until three in the afternoon. The ceremony was taking place in a tent just below the Riptide's deck.

The kids would go over to my parents' this afternoon

while I went to the wedding, but for now, I could enjoy having a lazy weekend breakfast with them. We made silly pancakes, eggs and bacon and giggled over the faces Cameron made out of his food.

I began getting ready for the wedding not long after breakfast. I'd found my dress at a local vintage store, and I absolutely loved it. The bodice was fitted green silk, setting off my hair and skin, flaring out into a full skirt. It was fun and flirty, and I was excited to wear it.

I was even more excited for Cooper to see it. Or rather to see me in it.

I dropped the children with my mom and dad, stopping long enough for them to admire me, and then I parked at the Hawthorne House so I could walk to the wedding with Abby. She looked elegant in her fitted silk dress, with a wide-brimmed hat to keep the sun from her pale skin.

"You look like a movie star from the fifties." I admired her outfit. "That's it, you're not allowed to sit near me. You'll steal all the men."

Abby laughed. "No worries, Em. No one will even see me when they get a load of you. Yowza."

"Yowza? What's that?"

She shrugged. "It means, like . . . hot mama! Or wooo hooo."

"Uh huh. You Yankees and your weird sayings."

Abby smirked. "Well, bless your heart."

I stuck out my tongue at her. "Bite me, Yankee."

We arrived at the beach setting in plenty of time. A huge white tent filled with chairs awaited us, and when we reached it, stepping down the wooden walkway set up for the wedding, an usher showed us to our seats.

The bride's side was filled with Cove folks, along with some of Jude's family from around the country. I recognized her Uncle John, the one from New Jersey who made and bottled his own limoncello and sent Jude a case every Christmas. It was good stuff.

The groom's side didn't lack for guests, either. I wondered if Burton, Georgia, had emptied out for this event. There couldn't have been too many left at home, for sure. I spied Alex Nelson, who darted over to give me a quick hug. I turned to introduce him to Abby, but she gave me a mysterious smile.

"We've met. Nice to see you again, Alex."

"You, too, gorgeous. How're tricks at the B and B?"

"Still running to capacity."

"Good to hear." Another man approached, slipping his arm around Alex's waist. "Oh, there you are. Emmy, this is my boyfriend, Cal. And Cal, you remember Abby."

"Of course." Cal offered me his hand. He was handsome, with darker hair that contrasted with Alex's sunny blond looks. "Nice to meet you, Emmy." He leaned to murmur to Alex. "We'd better take our seats before someone else does. And your mother's unhappy that we're not sitting down yet."

The two men joined the groom's side as the tent continued to fill quickly. Matt Spencer and his wife Sandra came in. She was glowing as only a woman in her second trimester of pregnancy could. They both waved to me as they took their seats. Eric Fleming and his wife Janet sat down next to them. Jude's brother Mark and his wife Samantha arrived next, which meant Cooper was the only member of the posse not there yet.

I resisted the temptation to turn around and watch for him, but just barely. The trio playing background music at the front of the tent changed tempo slightly, and the bridesmaids processed in. I pointed out each one to Abby, explaining who everyone was. When the groom, his best man and the minister came out, I finally spotted Cooper. He and Lexie slid into chairs two rows back from me. I kept my face to the front, afraid of what I might give away if our eyes met.

The music changed to Tim McGraw's *It's Your Love*, and there wasn't a dry eye in the house as Logan escorted Meghan down the aisle. I couldn't help glancing at Cooper. His eyes were on me, holding mine until I dropped my gaze to the floor, my heart thudding painfully against my chest.

The ceremony was beautiful and sweet. Sam and Meghan's vows to each other pulled at my soul. They each ended with the same phrase: *You are my first, my last, my only.*

I wanted Cooper Davis to be my last. My only. He wasn't my first and I wasn't his, but I knew that I'd love him for the rest of my life, no matter how he felt about me.

There was a burst of applause as the groom finally kissed his bride. We all moved to the adjoining tent, where tables had been set up along with a dance floor. I sat with Abby, Sadie and Mack, along with Alex's parents, Fred and Ellen Nelson.

"Such a beautiful wedding. We're so happy for them." Mrs. Nelson dabbed at her eyes. "We were friends of Sam and Ali's parents."

"It's wonderful that you could be here." I smiled.

"You couldn't have kept us away." Fred Nelson cleared his throat. "Now how about I bring all you ladies some drinks?"

Dinner was delicious—the caterers used our kitchen at the Tide, which was handy for this situation. Afterward, we all watched as Meghan and Sam had their first dance as a married couple. When the song ended and Sam kissed his bride with such gentle love, Abby sniffled into her napkin.

When the music began again, I danced a few fast songs with Abby, Samantha Rivers and Janet Fleming. And then the DJ announced that he was slowing things down, which was my cue to find a chair and rest my throbbing feet.

I slipped from the dance floor, intending to go back to my seat, when someone caught my hand. Cooper stood just behind me, rubbing his thumb over the back of my fingers.

"Dance with me, Emmy?"

I paused a moment before nodding. Cooper pulled me tight against him, so that my breasts crushed against the crisp cotton of his dress shirt. We swayed to the music in the dimmed light.

"You're beautiful tonight." He skimmed his nose down my neck to nuzzle behind my ear. "But then you're beautiful every night."

"Cooper." I tightened my hold around his waist. "People are going to see. And talk."

He glanced around. "It's dark, and no one's paying attention to us."

Pain rolled over me, a sting so sharp and familiar that I closed my eyes against it. I swallowed hard. "Cooper, I can't do this anymore."

"What? Dance? You're a wonderful dancer, Em." He kissed the top of my head.

"No, Cooper. I mean, this. Us. I can't do it."

He stopped swaying and stared down at me. "What do you mean?"

Tears choked me, and I struggled to breathe. "Cooper, I know you don't want to hear this, but I love you. I'm in love with you, and I have been for a long time. I tried not to be. Hell, I even went on a date, trying to forget you. I know you told me from the beginning that we can't ever be more than a casual hookup or friends with benefits, and I know I said I'd take it slow, but I can't. Not anymore. I love you, and it kills me to pretend I'm not."

I drew in a long and shuddering breath before I went on. "I'm not going to stop loving you, probably not ever, but I'm not going to cheapen how I feel by having sex with you and pretending it doesn't mean anything. The way you see us, we're like my piecrusts. Delicious, perfect, and exactly what you want, but temporary. Fleeting. I don't want temporary, Cooper. I can't do temporary. I need permanent, long-term, love-me-for-freaking-ever. And if you can't handle that, I don't want to see you again."

I pushed at his chest until his arms fell away from me, and I ran lightly from the dance floor. No one had heard me, and no one had noticed us, but I couldn't be there anymore. I'd make excuses to Jude in the morning. I stumbled across the sand and climbed up onto the sidewalk until I found my van. My old reliable minivan, just like me: nothing flashy, nothing anyone else would appreciate, even though it was dependable and safe.

I drove home by myself, shed my beautiful dress, climbed into my lonely bed and cried myself to sleep.

I was numb for a week, which was stupid and senseless, really, because nothing had changed in my life. I still baked pies and pastries, delivered them to my clients, and took care of my children and my house. I smiled and talked and interacted with everyone just as I always had. Nothing had changed.

And yet everything had.

For months, I'd been clinging to the possibility of Cooper's love like a lifeboat in a raging ocean storm. The idea that he did love me, and that he might eventually acknowledge that fact, gave me hope. It meant a bright and shiny tomorrow was out there, if only I could hold on long enough.

But now my lifeboat was gone, and I was tossed about in the waves with nothing to hold. Maybe if I'd never experienced the lifeboat, I wouldn't miss it, but I had and I did. Now the ocean was scary and dark and full of endless loneliness.

I went into the Tide on Friday night, watching the door while pretending not to. Season was winding down, and we were nowhere as busy as we had been. If Cooper had come in, I would've seen him right away.

But he didn't.

Saturday morning I woke up alone. I was determined to shake off this feeling, this pain, and I spent the day cleaning my house from top to bottom. I didn't forget Cooper, exactly, but I thought of him less and had a perfectly clean house at the end of the day. That was something.

The Tide was a little busier that night. We had a returning band playing, a group of folk singers from the Clearwater area. They were slowly but surely gaining popularity, and the crowd swelled to twice its normal size. I hardly had time to notice that once again, Cooper didn't show up.

I did close-up by myself, flying through the tasks as quickly as I could. It was past midnight, and I was tired after my cleaning frenzy and a long night on my feet. I set the alarm and locked up, happy to be heading home, even if I was by myself once again.

My house was dark and quiet as I turned the key in the lock of the front door. I thought longingly about my bottle of wine waiting for me and turned into the kitchen to pour a glass.

It wasn't there.

Frowning, I scanned the counters. Not one bottle. I began pulling open cabinets and even the fridge, on the off chance that I might've accidentally put it there while I was straightening up. But it was nowhere to be found.

An odd sense of unquiet seized me. As I closed the last cabinet door, I realized there was the glow of a light in the hallway. I hadn't left on any lamps tonight before work, and I hadn't been any place but the living room and kitchen since I came home. Someone had been in my house.

My heart began to pound. I reached behind the refrigerator and pulled out my trusty old baseball bat as I crept down the hall. The light was coming from my bedroom.

I took a deep breath as I turned into the room. My heart pounded out of control and my breath was erratic. When I pushed open the door that was standing ajar, I screamed in a moment of abject terror.

Cooper sat on the edge of the bed, holding my bottle of wine and two glasses.

I clutched the bat tighter in my hand, pointing it at him. "Are you out of your fucking *mind?* You almost gave me a heart attack. Holy shit, Cooper." I slapped one hand over my chest and staggered back into the wall, closing my eyes. "What the hell are you doing here, in my room, on my bed, holding my wine?"

"Well, I didn't come to murder you, so you can drop the baseball bat." His voice was dry, and I made a face at him as I let the bat fall to the ground.

"Then why are you here?" I managed to stand up straight, hands on my hips as I stared him down.

Cooper stood up, smoothing his hands down over the front of his jeans. He cleared his throat, and it occurred to me that he was nervous.

"Emmy, you told me you loved me. That you're in love with me, but that you can't deal with it, because you think I see us as temporary. What did you say? Fleeting, like a pie crust."

I nodded. "Nice recap for the folks at home, Cooper, but I still don't know why you're here."

"Getting to that." He drew in a deep breath. "Emmy, you're wrong. I don't see us as temporary. I see us as permanent. Long term. Built to last for years, for generations." He stepped to the end of the bed and pointed. "Like this."

There stood the most beautiful rocking chair I'd ever seen. It was simple; two sturdy rockers below a smooth seat backed by straight rungs and a plain headrest. The wood was oak, and he'd stained it light, so that I could still see the beauty of the grain.

"I built this rocking chair for you, Emmy. Because I want you to look at it and see us. When you sit in it, I want you to remember that I love you. Because I do. I love you, Emmaline Graham Carter. And I'm in love with you. I don't want to live another day of my life pretending I'm not. I want to be permanent with you. I want us to be a family, with your kids and my kid, and all of our crazy friends.

"But mostly I just want you. Forever."

I stood, with my hands pressed to my face. I was shocked to find that I was crying, rivers of tears coursing down my cheeks.

"Is that all you came to say?" I managed to choke out the words.

Cooper nodded. "That's it. Is it enough? I know what I'm like, Emmy. I know I'm difficult and moody and temperamental. I know I'm kind of a bad bet. But I'll love you with everything I am for all the rest of our days, if that means anything to you."

I took a step toward him where he stood by my rocking chair. Reaching out one finger, I stroked the top of the chair. The wood was like satin, but I could feel its strength and its durability. Its permanence.

I turned toward Cooper and laid my hands on his arms. Touching him, I felt the same thing I had in the chair. Strength, durability and permanence.

"It means everything to me." I whispered the words.

"Cooper Davis, I'll love you with all of me for all the rest of our days."

He pulled me down with him into the rocking chair, kissing me with all the promise and hope I could ever want for every single day of our forever.

The End

Playlist

Tonight Looks Good On You-Jason Aldean

Beside Me-Jo Dee Messina

X's and O's-Trisha Yearwood

Panama-Van Halen

Dead or Alive-Bon Jovi

A Little Bit Stronger-Sara Evans

She's Country-Jason Aldean

Rock of Ages-Def Leppard

Why Can't This Be Love-Van Halen

Acknowledgements

A well-known fact among writers is that characters don't just live within the pages while we're writing the story. In fact, they exist before and after, and their lives go on in our minds when the story on the pages is finished. So it was with everyone from Crystal Cove.

When I wrote *The Posse* two years ago, it was my first foray into contemporary romance (after paranormal), writing for adults (not for young adults!). It was scary, but as I have often said, Jude's story fell into my lap fully-formed, and I loved it. After it was done, I was fairly certain Emmy would have a book. But I got sidetracked by a group of college kids in South Jersey, and then by Rafe and Nell—oh, and then there was little town in Georgia and Meghan's story.

When we were planning this year's releases, I was giddy about coming back to the Cove. And they didn't let me down. Jude's been busy, cooking up new ventures, and the posse's been changing, too. Returning to this town and these characters was like a sweet visit with old friends. I hope you enjoyed it as much as I did.

So many thank yous to hand out, because the writing life is hardly a solitary one. To my regular, wonderful team, of course: Stephanie Nelson, who gave *The Posse* a new cover as well as created this one; Stacey Blake of Champagne Formats, who re-did her very first format for *The Posse*'s revamp and also made this one so pretty, as always; Kelly Baker, who keeps me on the straight and narrow by reading with a fine-toothed comb (yes, you will get more Alex!); Jade Eby, Emerald O'Brien and Maria Clark, who help me find order amidst chaos; and of course, Mandie, who cheers me on every step.

Big love to all my author friends who share the journey and speak the same language, especially Olivia Hardin, Gail Priest, Melissa Lummis and Christine Gomez.

And as always, to my patient family for all their humor and love.

Special kisses and hearts to my Temptresses. Y'all make me smile, and every day, you make my job my joy.

About the Author

Photo: Heather Batchelder

Tawdra Kandle writes romance, in just about all its forms. She loves unlikely pairings, strong women, sexy guys, hot love scenes and just enough conflict to make it interesting. Her books include new adult and adult contemporary romance; under the pen name Tamara Kendall, she writes paranormal romance, and under the pen name Tessa Kent, she writes erotic romance. Tawdra lives in central Florida with her husband, two sweet pups and too many cats. Assorted grown children and a perfect granddaughter live nearby. And yeah, she rocks purple hair.

Other Books

For more information on Tawdra's books and buy links to all vendors, please visit Tawdra's website at tawdrakandle.com.

Diagnosis: Love Medical Romances

Pretend You're Mine

Informed Consent

Internal Fixation

Intensive Care

Implicit Memory

Til We Part

Intentional Grounding

Ineligible Receiver

Illegal Touching

The Anti-Cinderella Chronicles

The Anti-Cinderella

The Anti-Cinderella Takes London

The Anti-Cinderella Conquers the World

The Anti-Cinderella Royal Romance Box Set

The Anti-Cinderella World Romances

Fifty Frogs

Hot Off The Press

The Cuffing Season

A Dozen Dreams (Coming Soon!)

Sort of Sleeping Beauty (Coming Soon!)

Slightly Snow White (Coming Soon!)

Love in a Small Town

Love Me Home (A LIAST Prequel)

The Last One

The First One

The Only One

The Perfect One

The Wild One

The Always One

The Hard One

My One and Always

The Forever One

The Love Song One

The Meant To Be One

Love in a Small Town Volume I

Love in a Small Town Volume II

A Year of Love in a Small Town
A New Year in a Small Town
Be My Valentine in a Small Town
My Lucky Day in a Small Town
Hoppy Easter in a Small Town
May You Be Mine in a Small Town
My Big Fat Prom Date in a Small Town
Make Me See Fireworks in a Small Town
Fall in Love in a Small Town
Be My Boo in a Small Town
Thankful for You in a Small Town
Merry and Bright in a Small Town

Crystal Cove Romances
The Posse
The Plan
The Path
Underneath My Christmas Tree
The Problem
The Crystal Cove Romance Box Set

The Keeping Score Trilogy
Young (A Keeping Score Prequel)
False Start
Three & Out
The Comeback Route
The Keeping Score Box Set

Making the Score Series
Down By Contact
Next Man Up
Game of Inches

The Career Soldier Series
Maximum Force
Temporary Duty
Hitting the Silk
Zone of Action
Damage Assessment
Scheme of Maneuver
Evergreen
Army Blue
The Career Soldier Collection
The Mustang (West Point Tour of Duty)
The Rotorhead (West Point Tour of Duty)
The Shavetail (West Point Tour of Duty)

The Perfect Dish Romances
Best Served Cold
Just Desserts
I Choose You
Just Roll With It

Books Written As Tessa Kent

Good Vibrations
More Than Words
Baby, I'm Yours
Save It For Me

Small Town Swingers
Welcome to Paradise
Night Moves
The Heat Is On
Fading Into You

Third Date Rule Romances
Crush
Crave
Crescendo
Tease
Tempt
Take

Tiny Bit Taboo
The Conference Taboo
The Ex In-Law Taboo
The Business Trip Taboo
The Client Taboo

Books Written as Tamara Kendall

The King Quartet (Young Adult)
Fearless
Breathless
Restless
Endless
The King Series Box Set

Serendipity
Undeniable
Stardust on the Sea
Unquenchable
The Shadow Bells
Moonlight on the Meadow
The Fox's Wager

Recipe for Death
Death Fricassee
Unforgettable
Death A La Mode
Death Over Easy
The Recipe for Death Box Set
Age Of Aquarius
The Save Tomorrow Collection

Printed in Great Britain
by Amazon

43860430R00126